SHADOW WATCHER

A Novel by

Michael B. Druxman

Other Books by

Michael B. Druxman

(2006)

<u>Fiction</u>

NOBODY DROWNS IN MINERAL LAKE

CHEYENNE WARRIOR

<u>Non-Fiction</u>

FAMILY SECRET

(with Warren Hull)

THE ART STORYTELLING

THE MUSICAL: From Broadway to Hollywood

ONE GOOD FILM DESERVES ANOTHER

CHARLTON HESTON

MERV

MAKE IT AGAIN, SAM

BASIL RATHBONE: His Life and His Films

PAUL MUNI: His Life and His Films

This is a work of fiction. Any resemblance to actual events or persons, living or dead, is purely coincidental.

For my wife,
SANDY
Who brightens by life every day.

CHAPTER ONE

He was being set up.

Charlie sensed it the minute he'd entered the hotel. There were no visible signs of danger. Nobody in the lobby appeared to be watching him while pretending to read a newspaper. No Feds in trench coats could be seen lurking behind the marble pillars. But, he *was* being set up.

His eyes searched the lobby bar for Brenda. She would've been here for thirty minutes now, and if something were amiss, she'd have noticed it.

Brenda was the perfect lookout...especially in these stylish downtown hotels that catered to the visiting businessman. Attired, as she always was, by the newest boutique on Los Angeles' Melrose Avenue and with a face and hair style that often had people thinking she could be Elizabeth Taylor's twenty-something-year-old granddaughter, Brenda could ensconce herself for hours without anyone...with the possible exception of a house detective on the prowl for hookers...taking any real notice. For *that* contingency, she carried an attaché case filled with documents.

She was seated on a sofa near the piano bar, wearing a slim beige suit that contrasted with her raven black hair and nursing along a Perrier. He didn't know the beanpole next to her, but by the way the guy was coming on to her, Charlie figured that he was one of Dallas' rising young junior executives...out to get laid before he went home to wife and kids.

He caught Brenda's eye, as she forced herself to laugh at one of Beanpole's jokes. The shake of her head was slight, and she covered that by lighting a cigarette. The signal was passed: "All was clear."

Charlie wasn't sure. Brenda had never let him down. He trusted her. But, something *was* wrong. His gut told him so. He trusted his gut more.

He looked at the people filling the lobby bar...the three-piece suits with briefcases attached...the secretaries trying not to look too blowzy after a day's toil. They buzzed and babbled at every table...on every sofa... almost drowning out the busty blonde in the red dress who was trying to play "Don't Cry for Me Argentina" on the piano, and the broad shouldered, balding fellow with checked sports coat and aviator glasses who was trying to sing it in his Louisiana baritone.

Nothing looked unusual to Charlie. Not even himself. *He* was in disguise. He felt uncomfortable, but for this trip, Charlie had stowed his favorite jeans and polo shirt and forced himself to don the three-piece uniform of the business world. His brown hair was shorter and freshly styled; his beard trimmed. With an official-looking attache´ case in hand, he no longer looked like a cocky, weight-conscious five-foot-eight Hollywood hustler, but was virtually indistinguishable from any other 28-year-old corporate hot-shot.

Indeed, when he'd looked at himself in the mirror that morning, he thought that if he lost the beard, he could almost double for Tom Cruise in *Jerry Maguire*.

Why, he pondered briefly, did everybody...even himself...remind him of some movie star? Oh, well....

Charlie left the lobby bar and strolled toward the house phones. He was still looking for that glitch that would confirm the warning from his gut.... *Nothing*. He took a chew from his fingernail.

"*Leave*," he said to himself. "Walk right out of the hotel and go back to Los Angeles."

But, there was twenty grand waiting for him upstairs. That was too big a prize to abandon for a hunch.

A four-year-old boy in a faded *Shrek the 3rd* T-shirt brushed by him, racing for the gift shop across the lobby. His plumpish mother was in close pursuit.

"Randy," she shouted, "I'm going to start counting!"

"*One*!" the kid yelled, not bothering to look back.

Charlie picked up the house phone. "Howard Loy's room, please." The phone was answered halfway through the first ring. "Hiya, Howie."

"That you, Powers?" Loy's accent was definitely West Texas.

"You expecting somebody else?"

"Nobody else knows I'm here." His voice was uneasy. "I'm in 823."

"*Run*!" Charlie heard his gut shout. "Get out before it's too late!"

"I'll be right up." He hung up the house phone and headed for the elevators.

Hal Stuart finished singing "Don't Cry for Me Argentina" with a flourish, and then gulped down the rest of his *7-Up*. Actually, there was also a splash of *Jim Beam* in the glass, but since he was on duty, he was *officially* drinking *7-Up*. From his stool at the piano bar, he watched Charlie Powers step into the elevator and the doors close behind him.

He took off the aviator glasses and stuck them into his pocket. Damn, they hurt his eyes. But, they'd done their job. They'd kept Powers from recognizing him.

"Where you goin', Louisiana?" The pretty blonde at the piano winked at him as he slid off the stool.

"Gotta make a phone call." He stuck a dollar into the tip glass in front of her. "You play good."

"You *sing* like Howard Keel."

Stuart laughed. He'd heard *that* before. Back in college, he'd even done the late MGM film star's roles in school productions of *Show Boat* and *Kiss Me Kate*. His drama professor had suggested that he was good enough to turn professional, but his father was against it. *He* was determined that his son would finish college and law school, and then join him as an agent with the F.B.I. Hal didn't like to disappoint his father.

He was thirty-five now and never really regretted joining the Bureau...even though his long hours on the job and, ultimately, that canceled cruise to the Caribbean, were probably the reasons why Helen had divorced him last year.

It was stimulating work. These copyright cases might not have much to do with protecting the nation from violent criminals, but they kept the old mental juices flowing, and the perpetrators seldom, if ever, took a shot at him.

Yet, in recent months...when he was home alone in his one-bedroom apartment...he couldn't help wondering if, perhaps, he *could* have had a successful show business career.

Maybe that was the reason he detested Charlie Powers. Why he'd flown in from Los Angeles to make this bust himself.

While the pianist struck up a chorus of "Make Believe" from *Show Boat* as his exit music, Stuart crossed the lobby to the registration desk. A black clerk was shuffling a stack of reservation cards, in an attempt to appear busy.

"He just went up," Stuart announced, dropping the Louisiana drawl.

The clerk grinned. "Let's go get 'im."

Charlie stepped off the elevator, humming his favorite song...the March theme from *Raiders of the Lost Ark*. He checked the wall placard for *823*, then turned left.

He was glad he'd decided to conduct his business in this hotel. If something went wrong, there were plenty of exits and plenty of crowds in which he could get lost. He recalled the time that he'd ducked the Feds at Dodger Stadium by swiping the coat and tray of a popcorn vendor, then selling the junk food all the way out of the ballpark. He'd picked up an extra eight bucks that way. Yeah, big places...with *lots of people* were certainly the safest.

He gave himself another oral manicure. The one time when he *had* been caught was when he'd violated that rule. His contact at the studio had insisted on meeting him late one night in a garage...two blocks from the old Columbia Studios on Gower.   "Nobody knows about the place," the jerk-off had assured him.

The Feds were *waiting* for them. They'd been following the bastard for weeks...hoping to nail him and whomever he was dealing with. Just as Charlie had stepped outside the garage, carrying a brand new print of *The Incredibles*...two weeks before it was to open in the theaters...the bright lights were turned on in his face and he heard that classic movie line: "*Freeze*!"

Miles Goodman was a good lawyer and had beaten the rap for him. Something about an improper warrant. But, the Feds knew who he was now. He had to play it careful.

His gut tightened on him again. *"Go! It's not safe!"*

He knocked on the door marked *823*. "Cute," he thought, "how they paint those little flower things on the room numbers."

Howard Loy was in his late forties. Charlie always thought that he had a figure like a fat pear and surmised that he dressed it in the finest clothes he could buy at Wal-Mart. He'd probably bought his hairpiece there, too.

"Hiya, Howie." Charlie assumed his cocky guise.

Loy took a quick look down the corridor. "Come on in before somebody sees you."

"Don't worry. They'll probably just think we're going to engage in homosexual activities."

Loy shut the door and locked it. "I don't know why we didn't meet out by the airport."

"This is classier."

"Cost me a hundred-fifty bucks."

"Then, make use of it," Charlie said. "Mess the bed up...take a shower...jerk off."

"Fuck you!" Loy laughed. It was a nervous laugh. He crossed over to the king-sized bed and pulled down the velour spread. "Satisfied?"

"Now, you're *living*."

Loy leaned back against the headboard and lit a cigarette. "Charlie, I know you're trying to be careful...but this cloak and dagger stuff is *dumb*."

"Maybe."

"What do ya got fer me?"

Powers set his attaché case down on the dresser and opened it. He took out two Digibeta tape cassettes and tossed them onto the bed. "Here you are, *sweetheart*," he said, lapsing into a fair impression of his all-time movie idol, Humphrey Bogart from *The Maltese Falcon*. "The stuff that dreams are made of...."

Charlie thought that Loy's eyes would pop out when he saw the labels on the tapes.

"Tell the truth," Rex said, putting his paw on Brenda's knee for the third time. "You really *are* her granddaughter, *aren't* you?"

She looked past the one-time basketball player in blue pinstripe, who was sitting next to her without invitation, and brushed his hand away like it was a gnat. "Okay, you win," she lied. "I'm am her granddaughter."

"Thought so!" His guffaw was triumphant. "Who's your grandfather? Richard Burton?"

"Granny's had *so many* husbands, I'm not really sure." While Rex struggled with that one, Brenda took the last sip of her Perrier and kept watching the activity over by the elevators.

She'd been aware of the baritone at the piano bar ever since she'd planted herself on the sofa forty-five minutes ago. She hadn't paid him much mind, figuring that, with the checked sports jacket and bright yellow tie he was wearing, he was probably one of those good ol' boys from the Louisiana off-shore oil fields who was in Dallas to peddle his wares to one of the corporate giants.

But, right after Charlie had left the bar area and gone upstairs, the guy seemed to change. He stopped acting the redneck and sobered up fast. She thought it odd the way he'd hurried over to the front desk and conferred with that black clerk. And, now the two men were standing in front of the elevators. The baritone had his hand in front of his mouth, as if he were talking into a cell phone.

"How about something a little stronger, honey?" Before she could answer, Rex had flagged the waitress. "Bring the lady a Double Martini."

Brenda stood up. "I've got to make a phone call."

"You're comin' back, aren't you?" He was beginning to slur his words.

"Of course." She straightened her dress and picked up her attaché case. "I want to hear about *your* grandmother."

Before he could reply, she was out of the bar area and on her way to the house phones. "Damn you, Charlie," she muttered to herself. "Why do you keep getting me into these things?"

Billy Lee Davis hated working hotel surveillances. Instead of getting to sit at the bar and play customer, he was always cast in the role of the bellman or the desk clerk... and not because he was black. He was experienced. He knew the hotel routine. Football had covered his tuition back at the University of Missouri, but bell-hopping had paid his living expenses. He liked being an F.B.I. agent, yet sometimes on days like this, he wondered if he wouldn't be happier practicing law.

"I don't know why you locals couldn't have supplied a couple of more men on this one." Stuart checked his watch, and then pushed the elevator call button again. "It would only have been for two or three hours."

"That was my boss' decision," Billy Lee said.

"If Powers gets off that floor, we're in trouble."

"Relax, Stuart. He *won't* get away."

He turned to look at the pretty brunette who walked by him. He thought she looked like Liz Taylor.

"We've only got three of the six outside exits covered."

Billy Lee shrugged. "I guess copyright violations aren't as big a priority here in Dallas, like they are in Los Angeles. We don't have the movie studios breathin' down our necks every minute."

"It's still against the law," said Stuart.

"So is extortion, kidnapping., bank robbery, terrorism...," quipped Billy Lee. "We spend our time on *those* crimes down here."

Stuart scowled at the younger man, then pushed the elevator call button again. "This is a high class hotel," he muttered. "Why does it only have three elevators?"

The doors to the end elevator opened. A chubby woman stepped inside, dragging her squirming young son along behind her. Billy Lee recognized the kid by his faded *Shrek the 3rd* T-shirt. He was the brat who'd been running around, bumping into the hotel guests all afternoon.

"Come on! Let's make this one," said Stuart. The two agents hurried over and jumped inside the elevator, just as the doors were closing. Stuart beamed with anticipation. "Press eight," he said to Billy Lee.

Billy Lee reached over to press the button, but he was too late. The kid in the faded *Shrek the 3rd* T-Shirt had already beat him to it. He had also pressed seven, six, five, four, three and two.

"Aw, *shit*!" muttered Stuart, seeing that they were stuck on a local.

"I'm sorry." The chubby mother attempted a smile.

The kid in the faded *Shrek the 3rd* T-shirt giggled.

Charlie finished counting the hundred dollar bills, and then stuck the envelope into his inside coat pocket. "You're going to do good with that one," he said to the fat pear. "You'll sell five...six hundred copies off those two masters in Brazil alone."

Still grasping the Digibetas in his hand, Loy turned to him with a look that was almost admiration. "Tell me something, Charlie." He laughed to himself; shook his head. "This picture's not due out 'til Christmas. How do you do it?"

"We make these ourselves, Charlie replied with a raised eyebrow, "*before* they even shoot the movie."

"I shouldn't have asked," Loy shrugged. "You're quite the character, Charlie."

"How's that?"

"You're selling me these bootlegs of brand new movies, yet your whole frame of reference is pictures from the 1930s and 40s. Hell, my kids never even heard of Bogart, Gable, Cagney and those other guys."

"Makes you feel old, I'll bet."

Loy nodded.

"My dad used to show me the oldies on video when I was a kid," Charlie said. "They were the best movies I ever saw. A lot better than the crap they make today."

"But, not as profitable."

The ringing of the phone caused Loy to blanch. Charlie stiffened slightly. He stared at his associate for a long, hard moment, and then picked up the receiver on the second ring. "What?"

"You're about to have company," said Brenda.

"I'll see you downstairs." Charlie hung up the phone. He hadn't taken his eyes off of Loy. "Been talkin' to the Feds, Howie?"

"You know better than that."

"Yeah, I do," Charlie nodded. "Sorry." He scooped up the Digibetas and tossed them into his attaché case. "Better have your phones checked."

"Maybe *you'd* better have *your* phones checked."

"Maybe you're right." Charlie snapped his case shut and started for the door. "I'll let you know where to find the merchandise," he said.

Charlie hummed the *Raiders* March in time to his trot down the hotel corridor. His escape was going to be close, but well planned. That's the way he liked it. He'd noted that the door marked "Stairs" was only a few yards beyond the end elevator car. If he could duck through there before the Feds reached the eighth floor, he should be home free.

"Dum de dum dum...dum de dum," he began to vocalize the March. "No one better be on the stairs...dum dum...."

Stuart remained silent as the elevator doors opened on the seventh floor. He glanced at his watch...just as he'd done when the doors had opened on four, five and six. He looked over at the four-year-old in the faded *Shrek 3* T-shirt and, for a fleeting moment, wished that there was some offense he could charge the brat with. Preferably a *capital* offense.

Charlie couldn't resist the impulse. He hit the elevator "Down" button on his way to the stairs. The doors to the center car opened. It was empty.

Surprised, he quickly pondered his choices. The elevator or the stairs? *Eight flights* of stairs.

He knew from experience that the Feds never sent more than three or four agents out on these copyright cases. The "big guns" would be on their way up to the room, leaving only one or two men to cover the lower exits. And, there were *six* of them.

Charlie liked those odds. He jumped into the car and pressed the button marked "Lobby."

Stuart flew through the elevator doors as they opened onto the eighth floor. Out of the corner of his eye, he saw the doors to the center car begin to close. Charlie Powers was standing in that car, and the son-of-a-bitch was grinning at him.

"*Hey*!" The agent tried to jam his arm between the closing doors. Too late. The doors shut, almost crushing his fingers.

"Check the room," Stuart snapped at Billy Lee. "I'm going after Charlie." He dashed back onto the end car, almost tripping over the brat and his fatso mother, who were emerging from it.

Stuart reached over to press the lobby button and stopped. He didn't believe it. This *couldn't* be happening to him. The little shit had done it to him again. He'd pressed every button on the goddamn control panel.

Brenda was thinking about that new running role on "Law and Order," wondering why she was here and not back in Los Angeles preparing her audition scene for the part. She saw Charlie step off the elevator. He waltzed across the lobby to where she was standing by the Commerce Street exit and they ducked behind the marble pillar.

"Stow this in a locker at the bus station," he said, exchanging attaché cases with her. "Mail Howie the key."

"What about you?"

"I'll see you back in L.A."

He glanced around the pillar at the elevator doors. All three were still closed.

"I want to wait for you at the airport." Brenda couldn't believe she'd said that.

"Do it *my* way," he answered, giving her a quick hug. "Go home." He took a little nibble on her lower lip, and then pulled back when she tried to do the same to him. "*Somebody's* got to feed the dog."

"Thanks!" She felt like ramming the attaché case into his crotch.

"Besides," Charlie said, trying to recover from another of his *faux pas*, "don't you have an audition tomorrow?" He glanced again at the elevator doors.

"And I *intend* to be there," she said like ice.

"Great!" He gave her a quick kiss on the cheek, and then danced over to the exit. "Don't worry about me," he said with a wink. "I'm home free." He disappeared through the revolving door out onto Commerce Street.

Brenda crossed the lobby toward the Main Street exit. She paid scant attention to the Federal agent in the checked sports jacket and yellow tie who came barreling out of the end elevator, shouting into his cell phone. Her mind was on that audition tomorrow.

She was going to *get* that part. She was going to be a regular on a hit TV series...make lots of money...and pose for all the magazine covers. At thirty, Brenda Grayson was, *finally*, going to be *a star*!

Outside the hotel, the doorman hailed her a taxi. "Bus station," she said to the driver. As the cab began to maneuver its way out into the rush hour traffic, Brenda lit a cigarette and dreamed of the day that she would tell Charlie to go fuck himself.

Charlie took a bite from his thumbnail. His gaze was fastened on the traffic signal across the street. Damn, it was taking its own sweet time to change.

He was still in front of the hotel, and he didn't dare run. For all he knew, the guy standing next to him was a Fed assigned to watch the perimeter. If he bolted, the putz just might remember what his mug shot looked like.

Charlie tried to place the face that went with the checked coat and the Louisiana baritone. He knew he'd seen that Fed before, but in different trappings. Was he the guy who'd busted him that night back in Los Angeles? Naw, he'd had more of a ski nose and a jutting chin. Taller, too.

The signal changed to "Walk." As Charlie stepped off the curb and started to lose himself in a group of pedestrians, he glanced to his right. Checked Coat was emerging from the hotel. For a moment, Charlie thought he looked right at him. He quickened his pace.

"Look for the people," Stuart said to himself. "Powers loves to melt into mobs of people." He moved down Commerce Street toward the corner where the signal had just changed.

"This is Stuart," he said into his cell phone. "I'm at the corner of Commerce and Griffin, heading west. Where the fuck is my back-up?" He wondered when the Dallas branch of the Bureau had become an extension of the Keystone Kops.

The agent studied the twenty or so pedestrians who were crossing the street. Four or five of the men were wearing dark three-piece suits...just like Powers. He squinted; tried to get a clearer look at them. One of the men glanced over in his direction, then immediately turned away.

Was that Powers? Stuart moved forward. The man began to scurry away.

"I got 'im," Stuart announced into the cell phone, "and he's starting to rabbit." He dashed into the crosswalk and tried to maneuver his way around the wall of on-coming pedestrians.

"I'm about fifty feet behind you." Stuart recognized the voice on the cell phone as that of Barnsdale, one of the younger agents assigned to this operation.

Stuart reached the opposite curb. He tried to spot
Powers, who had to be at least a half block ahead of him.
"You'd better get over here, sonny" he replied to
Barnsdale. "Marathon runs are not my thing."

"No problem," said the junior agent. "I was on the
Olympic track team."

Stuart smiled. As he began to sprint down
Commerce, he thought he saw Powers reach the end of the
block and turn right onto Lamar Street.

Charlie dodged a white Rolls Royce and a city
bus, as he hurried across Lamar in the middle of the block.
Then, ignoring the chorus of horns that were berating his
jaywalking, he ducked down an alley and, keeping within
the shadows, slowed to a brisk walk.

He felt pleased with himself. Those two-mile
jaunts he took down Mulholland Drive every morning
were paying off. There was no way those Feds were going
to catch up with him.

He thought about Brenda. He shouldn't have said
that to her about the dog. After all, she'd switched her
audition date just so she could come to Dallas and help
him.

She really cared about him, and he was treating
her lousy. "You can be a real shithead when you want to
be, can't you Charlie?" he said to himself. He decided that
he'd take her up to San Francisco next weekend and show
her a nice time.

He jaywalked again at Austin and continued down
the alley toward Market Street. If he turned right, he could
catch a cab a couple blocks down on Ross.

He was almost to the sidewalk when he heard the footsteps behind him. Somebody was running. He spun around. About half a block behind him, some young guy in a suit was racing down the alley in his direction. He was closing fast. And, trailing several yards behind him, Charlie thought he spotted the character in the checked coat.

"*Shit!*" Charlie dashed out of the alley and headed north on Market. If he could make it over to Ross, he'd be in that old warehouse area that the city had renovated. There'd be people there. People arriving for dinner at those luxury restaurants. People riding over the cobblestone streets in horse-drawn carriages. He could mix with those people, and lose the Feds for good.

He ran the light at Elm. "You crazy, buddy!?!" he heard somebody call amid the screeching of brakes. Charlie kept moving.

He looked over his shoulder. The young guy in the suit was gaining on him. He didn't wait for the light either. He dodged around a Chevy and leaped over the hood of a Jaguar. "Where the hell did they get *him*," Charlie wondered.

There were two cabs parked in front of The Palm restaurant on Ross. The doorman was assisting an elderly couple into the first vehicle, but the second one was free. Charlie stepped off the curb, just as one of those horse-drawn carriages moved in front of him.

"Watch it, mister!" the driver snarled, reining his steed. Charlie grabbed the horse's bridle. He ducked around the animal and stepped out into the street.

He didn't see the tan Volvo until it was too late. The blast of its horn and the impact that knocked the wind out of him seemed to come at the same moment. He felt himself being thrown up into the air. There was a hard crack on his head when he landed.

He lay on his back, looking up at the faces staring down at him...a cab driver, the restaurant doorman, a couple in their thirties.   Their lips were moving, but he couldn't hear any sound coming from them.

A pretty girl with auburn hair was in the group. She was crying.

Checked Coat pushed his way through the crowd. He glowered down at him for a moment, and then said something into his cell phone.

Charlie's vision began to blur. His head began to spin with random pictures and words. His last conscious thought was Edward G. Robinson's famous line from *Little Caesar*:

"Mother of Mercy, is this the end of Rico?"

CHAPTER TWO

Charlie was dead.

He knew he was dead. There was no question in his mind about it. But, he didn't give a damn. He was having too much fun.

There he was. He could see himself lying motionless on the ground about twenty feet below him. Checked Coat was on his knees beside him, first massaging and beating on his chest, then applying mouth-to-mouth resuscitation.

"He must *love* doing that," Charlie thought. He wondered how the Fed would like it if he suddenly revived and planted a wet French kiss in his mouth. "With my dying gasp," he mused, "I could tell the son-of-a-bitch I had A.I.D.S."

He'd never felt any pain. There'd been confusion... apprehension...then, as he'd begun to slip into unconsciousness, a feeling of peace...contentment had settled within him.

The blackness had lasted only momentarily.

He'd started to levitate...slowly...gently...until he'd reached his present perspective. "What an incredible sense of freedom," he'd thought, enjoying the weightlessness of being non-physical. "Waterbeds have got *nothing* on this."

He'd looked at his hand with a passing interest. It had turned transparent. So, indeed, had his entire form. He was naked.

Big deal!

He didn't feel cold. He wasn't embarrassed, since nobody seemed to notice him anyway. And, it really didn't bother him that a thin white cord was extending out of the back of his head down to the lifeless body in the street.

The circus below him was in full swing. The crowd of ghouls and gawkers had grown to where there had to be close to seventy-five people waiting around for their chance to get a peek at that poor dead slob. One old fart in a Dallas Cowboys cap was standing within three feet of the corpse and actually munching from a bag of popcorn. "Hell," Charlie mused, "I'm entertainment!"

He noticed the pretty girl with the auburn hair again. She was still crying. "What was she so upset about?" he wondered.

He thought it odd that he could feel so emotionally detached from what was going on beneath him.

The slim, well-dressed young couple dining on Lombardi's outdoor patio paid no attention to the event that was occurring across the street. Their eyes were fixed on each other's, as they enjoyed the bowls of minestrone soup before them.

Charlie swept down from his lofty position and hovered about two feet above their table. "What's the matter with you people?" he shouted, half-annoyed, yet half-amused. "I just got *killed* over there!" Oblivious of the phantom presence, the girl brushed a strand of blonde hair off her forehead and smiled at her man.

Charlie didn't enjoy being ignored. He tried to tip the bowl of soup over onto the girl's lap, but his hand passed through the solid object. "Couldn't Patrick Swayze do that in *Ghost*?" he asked himself.

He suddenly realized that he'd acquired a very interesting ability. He had the power to move in any direction...to any height...simply by willing it.

He glided over the heads of the curious to where a team of paramedics was now working to restore the late Charlie Powers. "Should've listened to your mother," he joked to his corpse. "Look both ways before crossing the street.

"Well, at least I'm wearing clean underwear."

Charlie was off. In his euphoric state, he zoomed up into the night sky like he had always wanted to do when he was a kid and had watched Christopher Reeve play Superman in the movies. "Faster than a speeding bullet. Able to leap tall buildings in a single bound...." He swept over the rooftops, his thin white cord trailing like a leash behind him.

The lights of traffic departing the city caught his attention. Charlie dove down over the Trinity River, following the Dallas-Fort Worth Turnpike west for a mile or so. The vehicles were bumper-to-bumper. Up ahead near the Fort Worth Avenue off-ramp, he could see the reason for this extension of the rush hour traffic jam. A Honda Civic had tried to cut in front of a Nissan Altima in the number three-lane. Two tow-trucks were trying to clean up the mess.

He headed north; back across the river and up to DFW Airport. He wondered in which of those departing planes Brenda was sitting. "Poor kid," he thought, as he hovered over the runway. "She's going to be real broken up when she hears about me. She's going to be even *more* broken up that I didn't let her take the twenty grand back with her." He decided that that was *too* low a blow. Brenda deserved better than that.

Charlie turned to see a Delta 747 coming in for a landing. It was heading directly for him. His first instinct was to zip out of the way. "*Fuck it*!" he thought. "What's it going to do? Kill me?"

He stood his ground...looked that jet right in the eye. "You want to play 'chicken'," he said. "I'm your man."

"Do not forsake me, oh, my darling...." He remembered the song from *High Noon*, and Gary Cooper's facing off the killers on that lonely western street.

The aircraft was fifteen feet away from him. Charlie decided *not* to tempt the fates. He shot up into the air and out of its path.

He laughed to himself, as he headed back to the downtown area. He was curious to see how events were progressing at the corner of Market and Ross.

From his twenty-foot vantage point, Charlie saw that one of the paramedics was about to insert an I.V. into his arm, while his partner, a girl with a turned-up nose and freckles, was using her radio to get instructions from the emergency room at Parkland Hospital. He couldn't help being impressed by the intensity in their faces. They were spilling *their guts* there just to save *him*. Charlie couldn't remember ever being *that* intense about anything.

The medic jabbed the lifeline needle into the vein. A barrage of flashbulbs exploded in Charlie's face. "*Shit!*" he muttered, anxious for the first time since he'd become an observer of his own demise. "What the hell is this!?!"

The blinding white light stayed with him for several seconds. Then, as it gradually began to fade, Charlie started to reorient himself. He discovered that things were not as they had been.

The street was empty...totally devoid of people and vehicles. There was no accident. His body was gone. Missing, also, was The Palm...Lombardi's. Indeed, the entire intersection had undergone a metamorphosis.

Instead of being a bright, bustling hub of Dallas nightlife, it had become a row of old neglected warehouses, dating back to the 1920s and before. The single corner streetlamp emitted a dim eerie glow over the area, creating baroque shadows in the door and alleyways. A large moth fluttered in front of the lamp. Charlie thought the giant specter it cast on the building walls looked like something out of a Dracula movie.

"This *can't* be the same spot," he said. He looked over at the street sign. It *was* Market and Ross.

He surveyed his strange new environment, hesitant to move down for a closer look. He'd never been into religion, yet he couldn't help wondering if old Beelzebub hadn't won him and was showing him his new home.

"What now?" Charlie asked himself, becoming aware that something else had changed. He shook his head...squinted. He was no longer seeing things in beautiful Technicolor. His vision of the world had turned into glorious black-and-white.

Resisting the urge to zoom off into the sky again, he started to hum the *Raiders* March, but discovered that he'd forgotten the tune.

Two blocks south, a pair of headlights turned onto Market and headed down the deserted street in Charlie's direction. As the car drew nearer, he saw it was one of those classic Cadillacs, circa mid-1970s. The vehicle slowed, as if the driver was looking for an address... or a person.

"What's he doing down here?" Charlie pondered.

The Cadillac crossed Ross, then continued by degrees until it was in shadow...just outside the streetlamp's range of illumination. It stopped next to the entrance to an obscure alley. Charlie could see that it was a blind alley that fed into the loading docks for a warehouse on the next block.

He glided down for a better look.

The driver had to be an ex-wrestler, Charlie figured, scrutinizing the robust man's muscle-bound posture. When he noticed his cauliflower left ear and the nose that must've been broken at least a half-dozen times, he corrected himself: "Boxer."

The man emerged from the car and removed a medium-size suitcase from the back seat. He had a full head of white hair. Charlie took him to be in his fifties and, considering the expensive pinstripe he was wearing, quite well-to-do. Then, he saw that the suit was twenty years out of style.

Charlie toyed with that. "Maybe he got it from the Salvation Army," he considered. "Maybe his boss gave it to him." He decided to let the issue pass when the man turned and revealed the right side of his face. A jagged scar ran from behind his ear down to nearly the tip of his chin. "Wrong again." Charlie started to laugh. "Welcome to *The Sopranos*."

"Lefty," as Charlie had tagged the hood, leaned against the car and lit a cigarette. He took a couple of puffs; checked his watch. "He's antsy," Charlie thought. "What the hell! I would be, too, in a neighborhood like this."

Charlie saw something move in the alley. A man stepped out of the darkness. He stood silent for a moment and watched Lefty, whose back was to him. This guy was probably in his early twenties, Charlie decided, and much more slender and better looking than the older man. In fact, with that strong jaw line, blonde hair and, in the dim light, what appeared to be blue eyes, he could very well be a fashion model.

"Naw," Charlie concluded, "He's a junkie and Lefty there is the contact."

There was something familiar about the newcomer, but Charlie didn't know what it was. He wondered why he was wearing an old trench coat, particularly on a warm summer night like this.

His speculations ended when the man slowly brought his arm out from behind his back. He was holding a double-barrel sawed-off shotgun. Lefty sensed the movement; started to turn. Before he could, the man pointed the weapon at the back of his head and pulled the trigger...both barrels.

"*Oh, Jesus Christ*!!" Charlie had never witnessed a decapitation. He'd never even seen anyone killed before.

Lefty's head shot across the street and slammed into the warehouse wall on the other side. It stuck there for several seconds, then fell to the pavement and lay like a red cabbage gone rotten.

The killer strolled around to the other side of the Cadillac, and looked down at the limp thing that was once a human being. Charlie could detect no emotion on his face. He was totally deadpan, as he broke the shotgun into two parts and stuck them inside his trench coat.

"Am I glad he can't see *me*," Charlie sighed, his initial shock giving way to a fascination with what was going on in the street below him.

The killer picked up Lefty's suitcase and walked back into the alley. A few moments later, Charlie heard a car engine start. The vehicle was a like-new 1976 Ford station wagon. It pulled out of the alley without stopping and headed south on Market. Charlie caught a glimpse of the rear license plate: "Texas, DYK 730." He decided to follow along for a while.

"What *else* do I have to do?" he reasoned.

The station wagon hung a left on Elm, heading for the Central Expressway. Gliding along about ten feet to its rear, Charlie couldn't help being amused at how these Texas hoods were into restoring 1970s automobiles. "Maybe that's where they're sticking all their hot money these days," he thought. Almost immediately, he dismissed the idea as being stupid.

He wondered what was in the suitcase. Drugs? Cash? "Wouldn't it be funny if it was the guy's dirty laundry?" he mused. He decided he didn't like himself for joking like that. The man, after all, was dead.

Charlie discovered that he'd allowed the station wagon to pull further ahead of him. He lost sight of it when it passed under the expressway. He was about to give chase, when he felt a violent jerk on the white cord that was attached to his head.

The barrage of flashbulbs exploded in his face again. His head became a top, as he felt a sharp, crushing pain in his chest.

Somewhere, he heard somebody say: "We've got a NSR!"

CHAPTER THREE

"You were very lucky, Mr. Powers." The baby-faced doctor made a notation on the chart, then replaced it on the hook at the end of the bed. "You're going to walk away from this with just a couple of fractured ribs."

Charlie didn't bother looking up, but continued to scan the pages of the *Dallas Morning News*. "When can I leave?"

"We want to do some tests," the doctor hedged.

"What does *that* mean?" Charlie felt one of his nasty moods coming on. "I want to get this fucking needle out of my hand," he snapped, pointing to the I.V. "It hurts like hell."

The doctor took off his glasses and wiped the lenses with a tissue. "Friday, *if* everything's okay. You *did* have a concussion, you know." His tone was not at all sympathetic.

Charlie didn't relish spending another three days in the hospital. He'd already been there for two. Actually, he'd been there for *three*, but since he'd been unconscious for most of the first one, he wasn't counting that.

He'd awakened in this bed with a head that reminded him of the morning after the time he'd passed out in the men's room of the Beverly Wilshire Hotel. He'd remembered being struck by the car. He'd remembered his strange dreamlike experience afterward...even though he didn't understand it. But, he had no recollection of how he'd gotten from there to here.

"Doc," Charlie put down his newspaper and motioned the physician to come closer.

"Goldstein." The young resident reintroduced himself to Charlie for the first time this morning. "I'm *Doctor* Goldstein."

"I'd like to talk to you about something." Charlie glanced over at Matt in the bed next to him. The forty-year-old, balloon-bellied school janitor with Spaniel eyes still had his leg in traction. He was still drooling over the newest issue of *Hustler*. And, he still had one ear cocked in Charlie's direction.

Goldstein glanced at his watch. "What is it?"

"Doc," Charlie said, lowering his voice a bit, "I had a weird sensation right after I got hit by that car." The physician's expression was noncommittal. "I thought I was dead."

"You had what we call a traumatic arrest." Goldstein seemed to enjoy pontificating his knowledge. "Your heart *did* stop. But, the paramedics were able to achieve a normal sinus rhythm."

"A *what*!?!"

"A NSR. They were able to get your heart beating again."

"Them paramedics are great," said Matt, not looking up from his magazine. "I watch them all the time on the TV shows"

Goldstein ignored the interruption. "That's why we want to keep you here for another few days. We want to be *sure* that everything's okay."

"I sort of figured the heart thing out for myself," Charlie said, embarrassed to get to the point. "But, what was *really* strange, Doc, is that I was 'floating'." He began to speak in a half-whisper. "I could see my body lying there. People were gathered around...."

"Sounds like *The Twilight Zone*." Again, Matt kept his eyes on his magazine.

"Mind your own business," Charlie snapped, wishing he were in a private room.

"Sorry," Matt replied somewhat meekly.

"What you described, Mr. Powers, happens to surgery patients every now and then," Goldstein said.

Charlie didn't appreciate his smug tone. It brought back memories of his fifth grade teacher trying to explain the principles of division to him for the sixtieth time.

"They imagine they're floating up in the air, watching the operation," the doctor continued. "Some people call it an 'out-of-body experience'."

"That's *exactly* what it was!" Charlie straightened up in his bed. "It was 'out-of-body'."

Goldstein's laugh was patronizing. "*I* call it 'hallucination'," he said. "The brain without oxygen can play some funny tricks."

"*No! It was real!*" Charlie felt his frustration getting the best of him. "I saw...."

" Mr. Powers," Goldstein interrupted, "you're upsetting yourself. Would you like a sedative?"

Charlie grabbed the newspaper and thrust it out at the physician. "*Damn it*, Doc, doesn't your lousy paper print the news?"

"What do you mean?"

Again, Charlie lowered his voice. "I saw a guy get blown away with a shotgun. I mean, *his head* went sailing across the street...." He paused for a moment to make his point. "There's not *one word* about it in the paper here."

Goldstein smiled again; rechecked his watch. "You *were* mumbling about that when the ambulance brought you in." He placed his hand on Charlie's shoulder and tried his best to sound sincere. "*Believe me*, Mr. Powers, it *wasn't* real. Truly, it wasn't.

"But, if you want to read more about this sort of thing, pick up the *National Enquirer. They're* always running psychic nonsense."

"Come on, doc," Charlie began to protest.

"Let the nurse know if you want that sedative." Goldstein was out the door.

Charlie couldn't decide who was the bigger asshole, Matt or the doctor.

"*'Twilight Zone*," giggled his roommate, his eyes still glued to the *Hustler*.

Charlie had his answer.

Under different circumstances, Charlie told himself, he would have dickered more with the insurance claims adjuster who visited him later that afternoon. He prided himself on that kind of haggling. Three years ago, he'd been lucky enough to have been rear-ended on the Hollywood Freeway by a very prominent Beverly Hills plastic surgeon, and that whiplash had earned him fifteen grand *without* the help of an attorney.

But he liked this adjuster. She was a ballsy redhead in a green striped suit, and she had an erotic smile. "My company doesn't like to litigate claims," she'd told him. "It wastes time and money."

"I agree," he'd said, waiting to hear her offer for settlement. He was thinking five figures.

"We're prepared to pick up your medical bills and hand you a check for three thousand dollars." She didn't give him a chance to object. "That'll save *us* the trouble of taking *formal* statements from the seven witnesses who saw you jaywalk in front of our client's car."

She'd been very persuasive. Charlie had signed the release form right then. Three thousand bucks was three thousand bucks.

After his nap, the nurse came in to give Charlie his dinner and to deliver two phone messages that had come in while he was asleep. The first was from Brenda, calling from Los Angeles to inquire as to how he was doing. The other was from a "Hal Stuart", who'd said that he could pick up his "belongings" at the local F.B.I. office.

"That *son-of-a-bitch*!" Charlie muttered to himself, finally putting a name to the Fed in the checked coat.

"Huh!?!" Matt, his mouth full with mashed potato, scowled at him. "You talkin' to *me*?" he said, spewing bits of food in his direction.

Charlie waved an apology. "Just talkin' to myself, fella. Sorry I interrupted your dinner." While Matt grunted and began to carve into his dried chicken breast, Charlie's recollection of Stuart came into focus.

Stuart *hadn't* been there the night Charlie had been busted with that hot print of *The Incredibles*. At least, he hadn't *seen* him there. But, on that day he'd spent in court, Stuart had been *very* visible. He'd been dressed more conservatively then...a gray suit...no glasses...and, he'd had a mustache. He'd sat at the same table with the government prosecutor and, when the judge threw out the case for lack of a proper warrant, a very clear expletive could be heard from that part of the courtroom. That four-letter outburst had earned Stuart a two-hundred-dollar fine.

"*Next time*, there won't be a problem with the warrant," the Fed had warned Charlie out in the hallway.

"*What* 'next time?'"

"There's *always* a 'next time' with you smart-ass punks."

That was two years ago. He hadn't seen Stuart since. And now, that bastard was holding his twenty grand down at the Dallas F.B.I. office. There was no *legal* way that he could keep it, but the only way that Charlie was going to be able to get his hands on it again was to go down there and answer some questions.

He considered calling Miles Goodman and letting him deal with it. Then, he remembered the size of the last bill he'd gotten from the attorney, and decided to handle the matter himself. Interrogations were like acting class. Charlie was a good actor.

"The money's in safe hands," he whispered to Brenda when she called again at seven. "All I have to do is go down there and sign for it."

"That's *all*!?!"

"More or less. Where's their evidence?"

"In a locker down at the bus station," she said without thinking.

"So, if this phone isn't *tapped*," he scolded, "we're home free." He considered telling her about his experience out of body, then, remembering Goldstein's reaction, decided that it might be better to wait on that one until he saw her in person.

"Hey, dummy!" Moe shouted from the seventeen-inch TV, "*Stop that*!!" He proceeded to bop Curly on the noggin.

Charlie shot an annoyed look over toward a thoroughly engrossed Matt. "Hey, dummy," he said, "I know you're a connoisseur of The Three Stooges, but could you turn it down, *please*?

The large man ignored him, then cackled with anticipation, as Larry let go with a pie.

"I shouldn't have called him a 'dummy'," Charlie muttered to himself.

"What?"

"Nothing," he said to Brenda. "You going to pick me up at the airport on Friday?"

Her momentary silence let him know that she wasn't. "I'm testing for that 'Law and Order' part," she explained. "I'm sorry."

"That's okay." He tried to sound enthusiastic. "Congratulations!"

"I play a real bitch."

"That'll be a challenge for you," he joked. Again there was silence on the other end of the line. He knew there'd be fences to mend when he got home.

"Mr. Powers?"

He glanced over toward the door. The pretty girl from the accident scene, the one with the auburn hair, stood there holding a vase of carnations and roses. Her tentative smile asked whether or not she was intruding. For the first time in his life, Charlie fell in love.

Her name, she said, was Jenny Bradshaw. She had light brown eyes; the softest, most caring eyes he'd ever seen.

Perhaps it was due, in part, to the pastel pink dress she wore, but a refreshing aura of innocence seemed to surround her. She appeared totally untouched by that "deliberate edge" most women he knew possessed. Gals like Brenda could be very passionate, devoted and giving...just as long as the relationship didn't interfere with their careers. The "Hollywood hardness" Charlie called it. He saw none of that in Jenny.

"Hello?" Brenda's voice interrupted his fantasy.

"Sorry." His gaze was still on Jenny. "The doctor just came in." He said a quick good-bye, then turned his full attention to his visitor. "Well, Miss Bradshaw," he smiled, "to what do I owe the pleasure of this visit?"

She appeared to procrastinate before she spoke. "I'm...I'm the one who hit you."

"That explains it," he said to himself.

"Explains what?"

"I was just remembering that I saw you at the accident. You were very upset." He chose not to elaborate about his unusual experience.

"I thought I'd *killed* you." The memory caused her eyes to moisten.

"You pack quite a wallop, but no cigar," Charlie said.

His light manner seemed to put her at ease. "I wanted to see how you were doing...to give you these." She put the vase down onto his nightstand.

"Thank you," he said, not wanting her to know that he hated flowers. They're very nice."

"And, I want to apologize."

"Hey, *I'm* the one who should apologize. I stepped right in front of you."

"I know, but...."

Charlie interrupted her protest with a wink. "And I'm only admitting that because your insurance lady was already here and gave me a nice settlement check." That worked. She laughed. "Did I destroy your car?" he asked.

"It's fine. How do *you* feel?"

"Very bored."

A loud guffaw from the next bed startled her. Matt slapped his hands on the bed, as Curly crashed through a paper Mache brick wall. "Don't mind him," Charlie explained. "He's writing his college thesis. It's called, 'The Three Stooges in the Nuclear Age'."

They surrendered the room to Matt, and Jenny pushed Charlie down to the day room. "When do you get rid of that?" She indicated the I.V. bottle hooked onto the wheelchair.

"The doctor won't say, but if it isn't out by tomorrow morning, I'm planning to mutiny." They shared a laugh. Jenny sat in a chair opposite Charlie and crossed her legs. "What does Jenny Bradshaw do for a living?" he asked, forcing himself to elevate his gaze.

"I teach third grade."

Charlie tried to act noncommittal. "Sounds...."

"Dull?" she smiled.

He liked her smile. "I was going to be polite and say...'interesting'...but if you want me to be honest, I'll say 'dull.'

"I appreciate honesty."

"What do you *want* to do?"

"I *thought* I wanted to teach, but I spend more time filling out dumb forms than with my kids." She pondered a moment. "I don't really know *what* I want to do." His warm silent gaze seemed to make her uneasy. "You're with the government, aren't you?"

The question took Charlie by surprise. "What make's you ask that?" he laughed.

43

"There were so many F.B.I. men around the other night."

"They take a special interest in me." The quizzical expression on her face reminded Charlie that he was talking to a "civilian," and, probably, an innocent one at that. "You might say I'm a traveling salesman."

"What do you sell?"

"Whatever's in season," he said with a shrug.

They spent nearly an hour charming each other. Charlie did most of the talking. He felt totally at ease with Jenny. It was the first time in years he felt he could be with someone without having to watch every word he uttered.

She was particularly fascinated with the tales about his father's pawnshop on Seattle's Skid Row. "Every day after school," he said, "I'd take the bus down to Pioneer Square and work until closing time. It was the greatest education in the world. These guys would come in to pawn their watches...their radios...their TVs....One wino even tried to borrow two bucks on his jockey shorts...."

"Had he worn them?" she laughed.

He chuckled and shook his head, indicating that he didn't remember. "My dad taught me a very important lesson during those years: '*Never* make the first offer. Let the customer tell you what *he* wants for his goods, then, no matter *what* he asks for, you undercut him.'"

"It must've been pretty sad working there," she commented.

"You couldn't let it get to you. We weren't running a charity. It was business. You had to turn a deaf ear to their sob stories."

"That's pretty hard, isn't it?"

"Jenny," he said with kindness, "so is life."

She wheeled him back to his room around eight-thirty. Matt, they were happy to discover, was already asleep. "Is there anything you need?" she offered, as Charlie maneuvered himself back onto his bed. "Anything I can get for you?"

He decided to take a chance and ask her. "Could you get me a book about out-of-body experiences?" Her surprised reaction made him wish he'd kept his mouth shut. He didn't care if Goldstein, Matt or even Brenda thought he was nuts, but he wanted Jenny to have a good impression of him.

"Why would you want that?"

"I had one." He tried to sound like he might be kidding. Jenny didn't smile. "You're not laughing," he said.

"No."

"How come?"

Jenny appeared almost relieved, as she placed her hand on Charlie's. "My father had one, too," she said.

Charlie felt a chill run through his body. It was almost a full minute before he spoke. "Tell me about it."

"It was about two years before he died," she said. "Dad was undergoing open heart surgery. He told me that he 'departed' his body...rose up into the air...and watched the whole operation from above. He even claimed that he passed through the wall and visited me out in the waiting room."

"How do you know he wasn't hallucinating?"

"I *saw* him. He was transparent...but *I saw him*."

There was no doubt in Charlie's mind that Jenny believed what she was telling him. He lay awake half the night with her words replaying in his brain. "If *she's* right," he thought to himself, "then *I've* got to be right, too." He tried to shift position in his bed. The I.V. in his hand made that difficult.

He wondered if anyone had seen him floating up in the air...transparent or not. What if the guy with the shotgun had seen him? And who was he?

He finally fell off around three, still trying to fathom why the killer looked so damn familiar.

CHAPTER FOUR

The book that Jenny dropped off the next day was called *Out-of-Body Experience and Beyond.* Professor Joseph Boyd, who was with the Psychology Department at UCLA, wrote it. Charlie, his I.V. finally removed by the nurse that morning, struggled through the first three or four chapters. He decided that he much preferred Stephen King.

Boyd's text described in minute detail a series of controlled experiments that he had undertaken at the university. Student subjects were observed in a state of sleep, then, when awakened, were asked to recite a phrase that had been written on a blackboard in another part of the building. The very few that could correctly repeat the words were considered good potential candidates for further testing, since it was quite possible that their knowledge of said phrase came by way of an out-of-body experience.

Skimming through the volume, Charlie came across several accounts of people, like himself, who had claimed to travel "out-of-body" while on the verge of death. In each case, the person had been without fear and had felt drawn to a strange, warm white light in the distance. Some reported seeing departed loved ones, who tried to assist them in reaching the light.

Charlie wondered why *he* hadn't seen the white light. Or, for that matter, why *his* late parents hadn't been there. "I know I wasn't always the greatest kid," he said to himself, "but they could've, at least, shown up to say 'hello'."

He skimmed a bit further, and then tossed the book aside, more confused about his experience than when he started.

"I see you're still here, Mr. Powers," Goldstein said upon entering the room.

"Where *else* would I be?" Charlie disliked the interruption to his intense train of thought.

The doctor placed his stethoscope on Charlie's chest and listened. "I thought you might be getting ready to drift out-of-body again," he said.

"Never on Thursday," Charlie quipped without smiling. "It's my day off."

Goldstein laughed. "That's very good." He put his stethoscope away and made a notation on Charlie's chart. "So is your heartbeat. I think you can leave us tomorrow."

"I'd have left anyway. I'm going crazy here."

"Just stay away from the psychic stuff, and I'm sure you'll be fine." Goldstein headed for the door.

"Doc," Charlie said, chewing on a fingernail, "before you go...."

"Yes, Mr. Powers?" Goldstein glanced at his watch.

"Tell me *seriously*.... The night I was hurt.... Are you *sure* there was no shotgun murder just a block or so away?"

The doctor put on his sympathetic guise once again. "Mr. Powers, ask yourself: If there *had* been such a killing, wouldn't it have been in the newspaper? On television?"

"Yeah...but I was *out of it* for a couple of days," Charlie protested. "I didn't *see* the papers."

"I did. There was *nothing*."

"Maybe they took the body away." Charlie and Goldstein both looked over at Matt. He didn't look up, as he glanced through the latest issue of *Penthouse*.

"What do you mean?" Charlie asked his roommate.

Matt appeared to speak with authority. "When the Mafia bumps off somebody, they usually take the body out and dump it in a swamp, or where they're gonna pour the foundation of a building."

"How would *you* know that?" There was a tinge of anxiety in Goldstein's voice.

"*Goodfellas* was on the TV, last night," Matt said. "Didn't you watch it?"

Charlie laughed. The asshole wasn't such a shmuck after all. "That *is* what they claim happened to Jimmy Hoffa," he said.

"It's possible," the doctor admitted. "But, if that's true and there *was* a murder, do you really want to get involved with those kinds of people?"

"Who knows?"

"I mean, we just *saved* your life. You're not a cat. You don't have eight more."

Charlie heard Goldstein's words, but they didn't stick. His thoughts were already racing in another direction.

"Good morning," Jenny said, as she entered the room. She was wearing brown slacks and a bright yellow blouse. Matt glanced up at her, and then put down his copy of *Penthouse*.

"Hi!" Charlie considered proposing right then. "I like your outfit."

"I always wear this when I play hooky. I like your outfit, too," she said, referring to the new gray pinstripe he was wearing.

"Courtesy of your insurance company. They didn't want me to go home naked."

Jenny giggled. "I think that emergency room nurses are frustrated dressmakers. They just love cutting off people's clothes."

"Especially men's."

"Beats *Playgirl*," she said with a wink. "You ready to go?"

"Yesterday I was ready." Charlie slid off the bed and they headed for the door. "Keep the faith, brother," he said to Matt, as he exited the room.

The head nurse waylaid the couple at the elevator and insisted that Charlie be taken out of the hospital in a wheelchair. "Hospital rules," she explained.

Outside, Jenny pulled her Volvo up to the entrance. Charlie climbed out of the chair, bid good-bye to the nurse, and got into the vehicle. "I appreciate your playing chauffeur for me," he said.

"I need a day off every now and then."

"Okay if we run a couple errands before lunch?"

"That's what I'm here for." She stepped on the gas, and the car headed down the driveway. "Where to?"

"*The Dallas Morning News*. I think it's on Young Street."

"What do you want to do there?" she asked.

"A little research."

Jenny knew her way around town. She drove right to the newspaper building. Charlie asked her to pick him up in an hour, and then disappeared through the front doors.

"Crime reporter?" The young buxom security guard thought for a moment, as if she didn't understand the question.

Charlie hated dealing with security guards and people in information booths, since none of them seemed to know anything. He tried not to sound too sarcastic. "You *do* have crime in Dallas, don't you?"

"Got my car stole last month," she replied without humor. "Is that crime enough for you?"

"Maybe you call him the *police* reporter here?"

She looked at a small directory on her desk. "You mean the guy that writes about the murders and stuff like that?"

"That's the guy."

The guard shook her head. "We don't have nobody who does that."

"*Come on*, lady." He felt his patience diminishing. "This is a big newspaper. Dallas is a big city."

"Nobody regular, that is." She didn't give him a chance to interrupt. "Mr. Wiggins used to do that."

"Wiggins!?!"

"He writes a column now. Don't you read the paper?"

"I'm from out of town."

"It's a good paper."

"I'm sure it is." Charlie was about to ask her if she even knew *how* to read, but then decided that might be non-productive. He forced himself to smile. "How do I find Mr. Wiggins?"

"Newsroom," she said, pointing the way.

Charlie took one look at Mal Wiggins and pegged him as an anachronism. Well into his sixties, the virtually bald, ruddy-faced and overweight journalist was seated at an old wooden desk at the rear of a newsroom filled with reporters with styled hair whose average age was thirty-three, and who wrote their copy at sleek modern desks and on the latest model computers.

Wiggins, a cold stogie clenched in his teeth, worked with an ancient Royal typewriter. In his unpressed, out-of-style suit with tie askew, he was, indeed, a character right out of *The Front Page*, that classic stage play about tabloid journalism in the 1920s, brought to life.

"What can I do for you, son?" Wiggins leaned back in his swivel chair and tucked his shirt back into his pants.

Charlie beamed his "nice young kid looking for a break" smile. "I was hoping you could tell me about a murder," he said.

"I know about lots of murders. Which one you got in mind?"

Charlie sashayed around the question. "I don't have the victim's name...."

"That don't make it easy."

"All I know is that it took place down around Market and Ross...and the guy got his head blown off with a shotgun."

The newsman chewed on his stogie, studying the cocky punk across the desk from him. The kid was putting on a first-rate sincerity act, but he'd met his kind before. They'd come into the office and pump him for facts on one story or another...usually the Kennedy assassination. Then they'd go off and write some book or article, make lots of money, and ol' Mal Wiggins wouldn't get so much as a box of cigars out of it. "Sounds like you're talkin' about the Vito Moreno killing," he said finally.

"Yeah?" Charlie's eyes appeared to sparkle.

"That happened down around Market and Ross."

"Why wasn't it in the paper?"

Wiggins stopped chewing. He leaned forward in his chair. "Are you nuts?" he said slowly...quietly. "It was on the front page for weeks. A.P. sent my coverage all over the country."

Charlie smiled; realizing that he was talking about apples and Wiggins was discussing oranges. "I think we're talking about two different...," he began, then stopped himself mid-sentence, hesitant to verbalize the wild, insane thought that had popped into his head. "Tell me, Mr. Wiggins, when did this Moreno killing take place?"

"You sure don't do much preparation, do you, kid?" the older man scowled.

"If you only knew the 'preparation' I went through to get the information I have. " He decided it would only confuse things to go further. "Please, when did it happen?"

Again, Wiggins studied the punk, trying to figure his game. "Close to thirty years ago."

"Thirty years!?!" He tried not to sound too surprised.

"You probably weren't born yet. What's your interest?"

"I'm writing a book on unsolved crimes in America," Charlie said, spitting out the story he'd manufactured in the hospital that morning.

"Book, huh?" Wiggins didn't believe him. "I'm gonna do a book someday...'Memoirs of a Crime Reporter.'"

"Sounds interesting."

"Do you know I was the only reporter to get inside Parkland Hospital when JFK got shot?"

"No kidding?"

"I was right next to Lee Harvey Oswald when Jack Ruby wasted him."

"Wow!" Charlie was impressed, but he had more important business on his mind. "I'll be sure to buy a copy."

"You do that, son." Wiggins glowered at Charlie for another moment, then began chewing on his stogie again. "Moreno's killing was definitely 'unsolved'," he said.

"Who was he?"

"Big shot in one of the local 'families'."

Charlie gave Wiggins a half-smirk. "I assume you mean 'Godfather' kind of families?"

"I don't mean the "Brady Bunch" kind." Wiggins leaned back in his chair again. "There were sure a lot of dead hoods around after Moreno got it. Touched off a real bloodbath."

"I'll bet."

Wiggins decided that he'd given away enough free information. "Go on down to the library," he said. "I'll have 'em pull the file for you."

"Thank you."

"What'd you say your name was?"

"Parsons...Al Parsons." It was a name that Charlie often used in conducting some of his more clandestine activities.

Wiggins waited until the punk had left the newsroom, before he picked up the phone and dialed. "Why should everybody else make bucks by picking my brain?" he thought. "Besides, a couple extra hundred would come in handy just now."

"Hello?"

The reporter recognized the voice on the other end of the line. "Let me speak to Mr. Moreno," he said.

CHAPTER FIVE

"Could it be true?" The thought raced through Charlie's mind as he headed down the hallway toward the newspaper's library. "Could it *really* have happened?"

The librarian was a Hispanic in her twenties. She handed him the Moreno folder and directed him to a table next to a row of file cabinets. Then she returned to her desk and continued clipping stories from that day's paper.

Charlie stared at the thick file on the table in front of him, almost afraid to touch it. "What if it *is* true?" he thought to himself. "What the hell do I do then?" He wiped his moist palms on his pant legs and opened the folder.

"GANGLAND CHIEF SLAIN"

The headline on the top clipping reminded him of something out of an old Jimmy Cagney picture. It made him wonder if the press borrowed their headlines from the movies or vice versa.

He unfolded the scrap of paper and looked at a photograph of Vito Moreno. The victim was in his fifties. He had white hair, a broken nose and, on the right side of his face, a jagged scar that ran from behind his ear down to nearly the tip of his chin.

It was a photograph of "Lefty".

Charlie felt no sudden surge of exhilaration. Instead, he felt cold, very cold. Several minutes passed before he resumed his perusal of the file.

The murder had taken place about eleven on the night of May 12, 1978. The operator of a city garbage

---

56

truck had discovered Moreno's remains the next morning. The man had taken one look at the decapitated head, and then thrown up all over the sidewalk.

According to the police reports, there were no significant clues. Virtually everyone in the Southwest with an underworld connection was brought in and questioned during the next few weeks, but there were no strong suspects.

Charlie paid particular attention to the dozen or so photographs that ran with the paper's coverage, including two or three shots of the dead man's widow at the funeral. Moreno's college-age son, Fredo, accompanied her. The captions indicated that the bereaved woman -- a blonde who looked to be in her early thirties -- was a former Las Vegas dancer. "Interesting," Charlie said to himself, noting that in none of the pictures were step-mom and stepson standing really close or comforting each other.

The other pictures in the file were taken over a period of two months. They were of Moreno's various business associates who were questioned by the police during the investigation. All of them, the paper reported, had criminal records. But, in their expensive suits, Charlie thought they could pass for members of the U.S. Senate. He didn't recognize any of them.

Why did the killer look so damn familiar? Charlie sorted his mental computer for the answer to that question. The reply came back, "No records found."

His eye caught a two-page biography of the dead man. Moreno was from New York, a former Albert Anastasia bodyguard.

Charlie surmised that he must have been off duty the day that poor Albert was gunned down in that barbershop.

Moreno had spent two years in Sing Sing on an armed robbery charge, then migrated to Dallas in the late-fifties where he was allegedly involved in the whole range of vices: gambling, prostitution and narcotics. With the backing of his New York connections, he'd built himself a powerful, well-insulated organization that was fronted by such legitimate enterprises as an Italian restaurant, a transportation company and even oil and cattle interests.

Moreno had been arrested in Texas only once. In 1969, a Houston drug dealer named Oscar Hopewell had been found in the Trinity River with his throat slashed. The local district attorney, who theorized that Hopewell had been encroaching on the wrong territory, came up with a wino who had been sleeping on the riverbank that night and claimed he'd witnessed Moreno do the knifing himself. The drunk described him perfectly, down to the scar on the right side of his face.

Two weeks later, the wino was run down by a school bus. The D.A. tried to make a case out of the coincidence that the bus had been leased from one of Moreno's companies. He dropped the matter when he realized that prosecuting the driver, a sixty-year-old woman with five grandchildren, would be difficult.

Moreno went free.

The bio continued: Moreno lived in the expensive Highland Park area of Dallas. He'd been a widower with one son when, two years before his demise, he'd spent some time in Los Angeles and come back married to the actress/dancer, Julie Joslyn.

Charlie looked again at one of the funeral photos, and wondered if the sullen young Fredo was fucking his stepmother without Daddy's knowing it, or if he just plain hated her. Maybe both.

The final clip in the file was dated January 5, 1984. It reported that Julie Joslyn Moreno had been killed when her Mercedes smashed into a telephone pole on Mockingbird Lane. She was alone in the car and had been drinking.

"Can I get photocopies of these?" Charlie handed the librarian five clippings.

"They're twenty-five cents each."

"You drive a hard bargain," he said with a wink.

The librarian giggled.

Jenny was waiting for him when he came out of the building. "Get everything you needed?" she asked, as he climbed into the car.

"Got a pretty good start."

"Where to now, boss?" She maneuvered the Volvo out into traffic.

"One Justice Way."

"What's there?"

"Your local F.B.I. office."

Jenny didn't say anything for a minute. Charlie could tell that she was choosing her words carefully. "Charlie," she said finally, "can I ask you a delicate question?"

He already knew the question. "Sure," he replied.

"Why does the F.B.I. take a special interest in you?"

"They think I'm a film pirate."

"What's a film pirate?"

Her naiveté amused him. "A film pirate," he began "is somebody who gets a hold of a copyrighted movie, makes copies onto DVD, then sells them to people

---

59

all over the world to watch on their DVD players. It's all very illegal. The studios claim pirates cost them millions every year in lost theater admissions."

She appeared to be confused. "But, you can rent those movies in a store, can't you?"

"*Before* they're released to the theaters?"

"Oh!" she said, seeing his point. The light ahead of her switched to green, and she turned the corner onto Justice Way. "How do you do that?"

"Most of the business is done out of the country," he said, ignoring her question. "Africa... South America...China...."

He was silent for a moment. "The funny thing," he said, trying to adjust the subject, "is that I don't really like many of the new movies. You can have your Brad Pitt and your Tom Cruise. Give me a picture with Bogart or Cagney any day over them."

"Who?"

"Let's say that they were the Robert DeNiro and Al Pacino of their day," he explained with a patient sigh. "Boy, do I have a lot of good movies to show you."

"Good," she said, then with a mock seriousness, "Charlie...?"

"Yes?"

"*Are* you a film pirate?"

His wide smile said he was invoking the Fifth Amendment.

Jenny watched Charlie enter the F.B.I. office and couldn't help thinking to herself that she really liked this cute guy. True, he might be dangerous; a "work in progress," but he could also be a "keeper".

"Stop with the bullshit, Powers." Hal Stuart scowled at the punk across the table, but held his temper.

"Stu, I wouldn't bullshit you," Charlie said with a look of total innocence. "How could I do that to such a great French kisser?"

"Humph!" Stuart looked away. He appeared to be a bit embarrassed at having given Powers mouth-to-mouth at the accident scene.

"Thanks for that, by the way." Charlie tried not to sound too maudlin. "My parents would've appreciated it." He glanced around the insipid room with its off-white paint and acoustical tile ceiling. "Hey, how come these interrogation rooms never have pictures in them?"

"Pictures?"

"Sure, brighten the place up a bit. I mean, right opposite that two-way mirror you could have a portrait of J. Edgar Hoover in drag...or something."

Stuart didn't laugh. Nor did he find it amusing when the punk stuck his thumbs in his ears and waved his fingers at the mirror.

Watching on the other side of the mirror, Agent Billy Lee Davis couldn't help smiling to himself.

"Are you through clowning, now?" Stuart asked.

Charlie turned to him and flashed a grin that the agent had come to detest. "I'm all ears."

"You know, Powers," Stuart said, "when an answer print from a big picture disappears out of a studio vault, then mysteriously reappears twenty-four hours later, you don't have to be a fucking genius to know what was happening with it."

"An *answer* print? Is that the opposite of a *question* print?"

—

"Don't play games with me, asshole,: Stuart said. "An answer print is the first print of a film that the lab strikes, so they can make light and color corrections….You know that."

"Yeah, but I wanted to see if you knew."

"You took that answer print and were making DVD masters off it. Digibetas."

"You prove it!"

Stuart got up and started to pace. "We know you were hoppin' around the country the last few days, doing business with your regional operatives."

"The last few days I was in the hospital, shmuck."

"*Before that!*" the agent snapped. He paused a moment to regain his composure. "If you're so innocent, why'd you run from us at the hotel?"

"I needed the exercise."

Stuart glowered at him in silence.

Charlie shrugged. "How the hell was I supposed to know who you were?" he said. "I didn't have my glasses."

"I didn't know you wore glasses."

"I don't."

Stuart felt his control slipping. His grip tightened on the top of one the straight back metal chairs. He was considering smashing it over Power's head, when Agent Davis entered the room with Charlie's money and attaché case.

"How's it goin'?" Billy Lee asked.

Stuart resented Davis' intrusion. He was also grateful for it. He turned to the punk sitting at the table. "Powers, " he said, "you're a very talented fellow. I saw you in a play once...."

Charlie hid his surprise. "Hey," he joked, "a fan!"

"Why don't you try to get a job *in* the movies, instead of trying to steal them?"

"Tell you what...." Charlie pondered a few seconds. "You call Paramount...Universal.... Tell them to sign me as the lead in their next TV series, and I'll be happy to stop whatever you think I'm doin'. I'll even go to the theater and *pay* to see their films."

"We got you once. We'll get you again," said Stuart.

"I'll look forward to it."

Stuart started to say something nasty, but Billy Lee came to the rescue again by tossing a large envelope onto the table. "There's your plane ticket and money. Count it."

Charlie picked up the envelope and started to stick it into his pocket. "I trust you guys."

"Count it, punk," growled Stuart.

Charlie held up his hands in a phony sign of surrender. "I'll count it. I'll count it." He took the currency out of the envelope and began to flip through it.

Billy Lee passed Brenda's attaché case across the table. "Do you always carry an extra pair of pantyhose in your attaché case?"

"*Pantyhose!?!*" Charlie was caught totally off guard. He could do nothing but laugh. "I see you guys found my secret." Avoiding the agents' hard stares, he quickly finished counting the money. "It's all here. Can I go, now?"

"Sign for it." Billy Lee handed him a receipt form.

Charlie scrawled his name, and then put the envelope into his pocket. With attaché case in hand, he headed for the door. He was halfway through, when he suddenly felt inspired. "Hey, Stu," he said, "are you familiar with the Vito Moreno killing?"

The agents exchanged a questioning glance. "Back in the late seventies?" Stuart asked.

"That's the one."

"I read about it."

"If I told you I could identify the killer, what would you do?" Charlie beamed the grin that the agent hated.

Stuart glanced at Billy Lee again, and then turned to the punk. "I'd have your head examined," he said with disgust.

"That's what I thought."

"Get your ass out of here!!"

Charlie could tell that Stuart was about to belt him. "Have a nice day," he said, and then disappeared out the door.

Stuart turned to Billy Lee. "I'm going to get that sucker," he announced. "I'm going to get him if I have to set him up myself."

CHAPTER SIX

"Oh, *wow*! Oh, *Jesus*...!"

Charlie fell back onto the bed exhausted. His mind mimicked a spinning top, as he fought to catch his breath. He now understood how a person could die during orgasm. All his life, he'd screwed... he'd balled...he'd fucked. Finally, he knew what it meant to *make love*.

Jenny nestled herself in the crook of his arm and pressed her naked body next to his. "Did you come yet?" she asked, as she stroked his beard.

"Maybe next time," he said.

She'd taken him totally by surprise when he came out of the F.B.I. office. "Where do you want to go for lunch?" he'd asked.

She'd leaned her head back and moistened her lips with the tip of her tongue. "My place."

"Her place" was a one-bedroom apartment in the University Park area. It had a skylight, lots of windows and was painted and furnished in an array of pinks and yellows that reminded Charlie of photos he'd seen in an old copy of *Better Homes and Gardens* that he'd seen in his dentist's office. A full wall of shelves accommodated her book, CD and VHS collections.

Charlie wondered why she hadn't yet switched to DVDs.

Jenny had led him into the warm atmosphere, then immediately began shedding her clothes, as she chose some chamber music to put on the CD player. By the time she'd reached the bedroom, she was nude. "What's keeping you?" she'd asked, as she pulled down the spread on the Queen-sized bed.

Charlie wasn't often at a loss for words. "I...I was watching you," he stammered, unable to take his eyes from her small pointed breasts. He began to doff his garments, picking up speed as he went. "I really didn't expect this." He dropped his shorts.

"I didn't really expect *that*," she smiled.

They'd explored, touched and, with delicacy, satisfied each other's bodies. They'd fallen asleep, and upon awakening, begun the process again.

"Do you have anything cold to drink?" he asked, catching his breath at last.

"Grapefruit juice, Diet Coke or beer?"

"Grapefruit's healthiest."

"Be right back." Without donning a robe, she scooted out of bed. He enjoyed watching her cute little tush wiggle, as it disappeared through the door into the living room.

The clock on the nightstand read five-fifteen. Charlie figured they'd have to leave soon if he was going to make his eight o'clock flight. He had mixed feelings about that. On the one hand, he'd never felt so close to anyone in his life. He liked that. On the other, his cock felt so sore that he was sure if he gave it any more activity, it'd fall off.

"You hungry?" Jenny called from the kitchen.

"You *did* promise me lunch."

"Tuna or egg salad?"

"Surprise me."

"I thought I already did that."

Charlie laughed to himself. Maybe it *was* best that he was going back to Los Angeles, he thought. He really liked Jenny. She was a lady who could tame him. He didn't know if he was ready for a collar yet.

He rolled over and noticed that he was being watched. Lying in the corner armchair was a small white poodle, its head resting on its paws as it kept its eyes trained on the intruder in its mistress' bed. "Hello," Charlie said. "You enjoy the show?"

The dog growled.

"I can see that we're going to be the best of friends."

Jenny entered, carrying a tray of finger sandwiches and two glasses of grapefruit juice. "I see you've met Roger," she said.

"Roger!?!"

"He's named after an old boyfriend."

"Is there much of a resemblance?"

"Some." She set the tray onto the bed.

Charlie popped an egg salad into his mouth. "I got a dog," he said. "His name's Odif."

"Odif? What is that? Swedish?"

"It's 'Fido' spelled backwards."

Jenny giggled. "You're silly."

"Really, that's his name."

With the help of Roger, they finished their lunch. Jenny snuggled back up against him and began stroking his beard again. Charlie found that his cock didn't fall off after all.

"Charlie," Jenny began when they were in the shower together, "what did you do before you became...an *alleged* film pirate?"

He gently sponged off her breasts. "I was an *aspiring* actor," he said. "I was gonna be the next DeNiro." His impression of the star was first-rate. "Are you talkin' to me?"

"What happened?"

"I got tired of parking cars at night and living in a firetrap down on Vermont Avenue. Making money is better for the soul."

She put her arms around him and hugged tight. "Do you really have to catch the eight o'clock?" she asked.

"I'll be coming back." He wanted to mean that.

His flight arrived at LAX ten minutes early. Charlie walked through the gate to find Brenda waiting for him. She was attired in cream-colored tank top and designer jeans, and her face wore the hungry look that meant he'd better prepare himself for an all-night session. The prospect didn't particularly excite him.

"I thought you were testing for 'Law and Order'." He forced himself to smile.

"We finished early," she said, planting a warm kiss on his lips. "I thought I'd surprise you."

"You did." He felt the softness of her pubis rub against his leg. Memories stirred below his waist. "I'm glad you did," he said with growing mixed emotions.

"How do you feel?"

He responded to her closeness and kissed her for a long moment. "You know how I feel."

"From the accident, you pervert."

Charlie smiled and put his arm around her waist. "Sore ribs. Otherwise, I'm fine." He stopped for a *Los Angeles Times* at the newsstand, and then they headed for the escalator and the airport's street level.

—

68

"How'd the test go?" he asked her.

"It's between me and three other girls. They're sending the film back to New York for a decision."

As Brenda turned her Corvette onto the ramp that would point them north on the San Diego Freeway, Charlie told her about his out-of-body experience. "The strange thing was that I wasn't scared," he said. "I mean, I really didn't care if I got back into my body or not. It was such a sense of freedom."

"Hon...." Her voice was one big question mark. "Are you sure you weren't dreaming or something?"

"I *wasn't* dreaming," he said, producing the book that Jenny had given him from his attaché case. "This professor at UCLA has been doing research in this area. I might even go see him."

"Why bother?" she retorted. "What's it going to do for you? Even if you did have an 'out-of-body' experience, that and a dollar won't even get you a ride on a bus these days."

Brenda's lack of enthusiasm was like a splash of cold water in his face. He briefly considered not telling her the rest of his adventure. "Jenny would've been more understanding...more receptive," he thought. He wished he had confided in her more. But then, he didn't want to take the chance of frightening her off. Out-of-body experiences were one thing, but time travel and gangland murders were quite another.

He looked at Brenda and figured if he didn't tell her, who else would he tell? "I saw something when I was out of body," he said as they passed by the Westwood area. "And, I really don't know what to do about it yet."

———

During their drive down Mulholland, Charlie gave her a detailed account of how he had witnessed the Vito Moreno murder. He turned on the car light and showed her the newspaper stories he had photocopied. She glanced at them, while he held the steering wheel and maneuvered the vehicle along the curving road.

"So, what do you think?" he asked, as she pulled up into his driveway.

She put the car into "Park" and turned off the motor. "Charlie," she said, "if a stranger told me what you just told me, I'd run for the nearest exit."

"But *I* told you."

"I know." She was silent for several seconds. "You'd been hit by a car. You were technically 'dead.' How can you trust anything you thought you saw?"

"I *was* there," he said, trying to repress his growing annoyance with her. "I *saw* the murder. I *saw* the face of the killer."

"And all this happened in the 1970s?" She forced herself not to smile.

"I saw the man, damn it!"

She opened her car door. "Can you identify him?'

"Yes."

"Who is he?"

"I don't know his name," he said, getting out of the car. "But you put him in a line-up or show me his picture, and I'll point him out."

Charlie had been leasing the house for the past eight months from an actor who was in New York doing a soap. Located just off Mulholland, the thirty-year-old, two-bedroom rustic was protected from the road by a row of tall spruce and was built into a small hillside niche, so that it commanded a majestic view of the San Fernando Valley.

"Hey, Odif!" Charlie knelt to greet the large German Shepherd that bounded up to him, as he opened the front door. "How ya doin', boy?" The dog squealed with delight and buried his snout between his master's legs.

"He missed me," Charlie said, as Brenda headed for the kitchen.

"He was really depressed," she said. "I think he sensed something was wrong."

"Were you worried about me, boy?" Charlie turned the animal onto its back and rubbed its belly.

"Want some coffee?" Brenda called out from the kitchen.

"Put some brandy in it."

Coffee was served in the bedroom. "I missed you," Brenda said, as Charlie dutifully removed her tank top. "I didn't want to miss you, but I did."

"I missed you, too." He tried to sound convincing.

She pulled down her panties, then, hands on her hips, scowled at the poster from *The Searchers* hanging over the bed. "Charlie," she said in a half-serious tone, "how many times do I have to tell you that it's not very romantic to make love with John Wayne looking down on you."

"I like that picture." He took off his shirt and laughed, thankful that she had lightened the mood. "Don't you feel protected with 'the Duke' standing guard?"

"I'd feel just as protected if he stood guard from the living room." She got under the covers. "Why don't you switch it with one of your other posters?"

"Let's see, " he mused, playing with that idea while he finished undressing, "what do I have that's more romantic...? How about *The Gay Divorcee*? That's a pretty poster."

"*Please*," she chuckled.

"I got a Bugs Bunny in the kitchen." He got under the covers and embraced her. "Or, how about *The Bride of Frankenstein*? What could be more romantic than a wedding?"

"Just shut up and fuck me," she said.

And that's what he did. There was none of the tenderness, the gentleness that there'd been with Jenny that afternoon. There was only their usual frantic by-the-numbers race to reach a climax. Afterwards, he'd felt empty, guilty that he'd betrayed Jenny and destroyed something special. Charlie didn't like himself for that.

He leaned back against the headboard and watched Brenda sleep. "She's just like a guy that way," he thought. "Let 'er come and two minutes later she's dead to the world." Unable to nod off, he slipped out of bed, put on a robe and went out into the living room.

Odif was lying in his favorite spot by the used brick fireplace. He looked up as his master entered the room. His tired tail was able to produce a single wag. Then, with a sigh, he put his head back down between his paws and resumed his sleep.

Charlie sat down on the sofa and put his feet up on the mosaic coffee table. He glanced through the mail that had come while he was away. There were a few bills. Some advertisements. Nothing important.

He looked around the room at the movie memorabilia that he'd collected over the years, and wondered if these things would delight Jenny as much as they did him. There were framed posters and lobby cards. A plaster replica of the Maltese Falcon was on his desk. And, one autographed piece was on the wall of which he was especially proud: an original window card from *Top Hat*, signed by both Fred Astaire and Ginger Rogers. He hoped that Jenny *would* enjoy them because, after tonight, he knew that he was going to make her an important part of his life.

"How can I do that to Brenda?" he said out loud to himself. He knew she could be a pain-in-the-ass bitch sometimes...like tonight in the car. But, she was also a good friend. His best friend. He took a bite off of his fingernail and prayed that she got the role on "Law and Order." That would make his breaking up with her so much easier, since the show was shot entirely in New York.

The long day began to catch up with him. He considered returning to the bedroom, but getting to his feet and walking that short distance suddenly seemed like too much work. "Maybe in a few minutes," he thought.

He picked up the copy of the *Times* that he'd purchased at the airport. There was nothing very extraordinary on the front page. Congress was still debating health care. The Los Angeles City Council was still arguing about a new sales tax. And the Dodgers had lost last night's game...again.

He finished scanning the front section, then tossed it aside and turned to the California section. The paper had devoted the entire first page of that section to capsule biographies of the four prominent Californians who had recently thrown their hats into the ring for the upcoming race for governor.

Politics bored Charlie. He was about to turn the page when he stopped and looked again at one of the four photographs.

"Oh, *shit*!!" The coldness that he'd felt that morning in the newspaper library returned, except that, this time, it was more like ice.

The immaculately attired man in the *Times* photo was older -- in his early fifties -- and he wore his hair in a different style. But, he still had that strong jawline and blondish hair that reminded Charlie of a fashion model.

"*I got him*!" he shouted, bursting into the bedroom.

"What!?!" A dazed Brenda opened her eyes, and then closed them again.

"Come on! Wake up!" He shook her until she surrendered to consciousness.

"Damn you, Charlie! I was asleep."

"Listen to me, Brenda. Read my lips," he said. "I can name the killer."

"What are you talking about?"

He thrust the paper in front of her face and pointed to the photograph.

"That's the man that killed Vito Moreno."

Brenda stared at the paper for several long moments before his announcement began to register. "You're crazy!" she said, mouth agape.

"*That's* who I saw."

"But, that's Bob Harlow!"

"Right!"

"He's running for governor."

"I know. Consider the possibilities."

CHAPTER SEVEN

Charlie phoned UCLA at nine the next morning and asked for Professor Joseph Boyd. The Information Operator referred him to an extension in the Psychology Department.

"Why don't you write down your experience in detail and mail it to me?" Boyd suggested.

"I'd like to come over and see you in person."

"I'm really too busy to meet...."

Charlie didn't like getting a brush-off. It was one of the reasons why he'd stopped trying to make it as an actor. "This wasn't one of your ordinary, run-of-the-mill out-of-body experiences," he said, interrupting Boyd mid-sentence.

"Few of them are." The professor sounded patronizing.

"Do most of them involve time travel?" There was no response from the other end of the line. "Hello?" Charlie wondered if Boyd had hung up.

"I'm still here," Boyd said, smacking his lips. "Tell me about it."

Without mentioning names, Charlie gave him a quick rundown of the murder he'd seen and the results of his subsequent investigations.

"Are you sure, Mr. Powers," the educator asked, "that you didn't just read about this case some time ago and simply forgot about it? Something like this could have been hidden somewhere in your subconscious."

"I don't think so."

"Okay, then," Boyd said. "Can you come over at two?"

Charlie was halfway through the front door when Brenda, still dripping from her shower, called to him. "You're not going dressed like *that*, are you?" she said.

"I always dress like this."

"Hon," she snickered, "if you go see him wearing jeans and a polo shirt, he's going to treat you like a damn student."

"I see your point." He shut the front door, and muttered, "*Shit!*"

"Wear your pin-stripe."

"I don't want to wear my pin-stripe," he said. "It's too uncomfortable."

"Life *is* a struggle." She disappeared back into the bedroom.

"I am *not* going to wear my pin-stripe," he said, starting for the bedroom. "I'll wear my blue blazer."

"Whatever you say."

He wore the pinstripe.

Considering the impressive string of letters after Boyd's name, Charlie had envisioned the professor as being a short, aged gentleman in a white lab coat, with hair like Albert Einstein, sucking on a pipe and sounding like a New England version of Anthony Hopkins. Instead, he encountered a thirty-five-year-old lanky black dude in a white lab coat, who shaved his head, sometimes chewed on the end of his eyeglasses and spoke like a California version of Orson Welles.

"We scientists refer to it as OBE, or Out-of-Body Experience," Boyd explained, as he led Charlie down the corridor toward the research wing of the Psychology Department. "The mystics call it astral projection or soul travel." He opened the door at the end of the hall and motioned his guest to enter. "Our research has been anything but conclusive."

They entered a large room containing a row of four sleeping cubicles, each with its own one-way window. Only the first chamber was lit or occupied. A male student of about twenty lay on the cot, apparently sleeping. A stout student with a handlebar mustache, who was stationed at a desk outside the small rooms, was monitoring his movements and sleep patterns.

"Hello, Hughes," Boyd said to the monitor without looking directly at him.

"Good afternoon, Professor." Hughes appeared uncomfortable, as he made a notation on his clipboard. Charlie thought he saw him hide something under the textbook in front of him.

"That young man is asleep." Boyd directed Charlie's attention to the student in the cubicle. "Hopefully, he will have an OBE during his slumber. Now, at the other end of this building is a research assistant who has drawn a geometric design on the blackboard...."

"I thought you used words...phrases?" Charlie asked.

"That was last year." Boyd punctuated with a smack of the lips. His cool stare let Charlie know that he did not like being interrupted. "This year, we're using geometric designs."

"I see," Charlie nodded dutifully.

77

Boyd smiled and went on with the dissertation that he'd given many times before. "If, when our subject awakens, he is able to duplicate that design, one might conclude that he traveled to that other room 'out of body'." He continued before Charlie could ask his question. "Of course, at this point, there's no way to tell if he had a *legitimate* OBE, or if he learned the information through some sort of telepathy."

"That kid may not be having a legitimate OBE," Charlie quipped, noting that there was a very large bulge in the sleeping student's jeans, "but he's sure having one fantastic dream."

"Yes." Boyd was not amused.

"My experience *was* legitimate," Charlie said.

The professor smiled briefly. "Ever since the tabloids picked up on this sort of phenomena, *everyone* is having legitimate experiences." Again he continued before Charlie could interrupt. "But that's not why I agreed to see you."

Boyd led Charlie to the other side of the large room, and a door marked "Private". As he unlocked the door, he turned back to the student monitor. "Hughes."

The young man looked up from his textbook. "Sir?"

"What are you reading?"

"The Rawlins text, sir."

"I mean *under* the text."

Hughes blushed and flashed a sheepish grin. He held up a copy of *MAD* magazine.

Boyd's expression remained deadpan. "Let me see it when you're finished, will you?" Then he opened the door and invited Charlie into his office.

Had Boyd exhibited a sense of humor, Charlie might have jokingly asked if they'd entered a storeroom by mistake. The windowless office was about the size of one, and with all four walls covered from floor to ceiling with filled bookshelves, Charlie found the room to be almost claustrophobic.

"May I offer you a Diet Pepsi?" Boyd asked, opening a small refrigerator in the corner.

"Sure. Thanks." Charlie plopped himself down into a chair. He decided that he'd better not joke about the professor's messy desk either. "I took a couple of Psychology courses when I was in school," he offered. "They were pretty interesting."

"Sorry, no glasses." Boyd handed him the soft drink, then sat down behind his desk. "Where did you attend college?"

"University of Washington. But, I was only in school for a year."

"They have a good department there."

"I guess so," Charlie shrugged. "I never really enjoyed sitting in a classroom though. I've always learned best by just doing."

Boyd didn't comment. He simply studied him for a few moments. Charlie wasn't sure if he should say anything or not. He smiled, crossed then uncrossed his legs.

"These days," the professor said finally, "my assistant does most of the interviewing. I haven't the patience any longer."

"You must get lots of nuts."

"Tell me more about this...'vision' you had of the murder."

"Then you believe it could be genuine?"

"I'm a scientist, Mr. Powers." Boyd's tone was almost scolding. "I require proof." He took a sip from his Pepsi. "But, one could argue that *if* we were able to leave the body and thereby enter another plane or dimension, then, while in that state, why couldn't we go backwards or forward in time? Some theorists believe that the past, present and future all co-exist in different dimensions. If we could only find the 'key', we could travel from one to another."

They spent over an hour in the cramped office. Right down to the killer's license number, Charlie gave the educator a candid step-by-step account of Moreno's slaying. He omitted only Harlow's name. "I got these from the local newspaper files," he said, passing the photocopied clippings across the desk to Boyd.

"Aren't you contradicting yourself, Mr. Powers?"

"How so?"

Boyd referred to some notes he'd been scribbling on the back of an envelope. "You state that, once you 'went back in time,' everything turned into black-and-white."

"That's right."

"How then could you tell that the murderer had *blue* eyes?"

"The same way you can look at Paul Newman or Frank Sinatra in a black-and-white photograph and tell that they've got baby blues." Boyd didn't seem to comprehend his meaning. "Shades of gray, professor."

"Yes," Boyd nodded, "of course." He scribbled another note.

"Thought you had me, didn't you?" Charlie said.

Boyd shrugged and did his best to smile. "In one of our testings a few months ago," he said, "the subject -- a freshman from Ohio who'd never been in California before -- awoke from her sleep and described this office. In particular, she described a figurine of a black cat that was on my desk."

Charlie looked at the desk, then turned and scanned the bookshelves. He didn't see a figurine of a black cat.

"It's not here," Boyd said. "It was accidentally broken and thrown away about three years ago. At least, thirty months *before* the subject said she saw it. *But*, it *had* been here once."

Charlie leaned forward in his chair. "Then, you're saying...."

"All I'm saying is: 'Isn't that interesting?'" The professor stood up, signaling the end of the interview. "Would you be willing to undergo a few tests?" he asked.

"Tests?" Ever since his school days, that word had always provoked a conditioned response from Charlie. "What *kind* of tests?"

"Tests to measure your level of Extra Sensory Perception and that sort of thing. The results might prove interesting."

"Will they hurt?"

"Not hardly." Boyd took an appointment book out of his pocket. "Would next Tuesday be convenient?"

"If I'm in town, I'd be happy to do the tests," Charlie lied. "Can I let you know?"

The professor scowled. "You have my number," he said, putting the book back into his pocket.

Boyd escorted Charlie out of the research wing and back down the main corridor toward the building's exit. "What are your plans, Mr. Powers?" he asked as they reached the door.

"To see if I can prove I saw what I saw."

"You say you *did* recognize the man with the shotgun?"

"Yes."

"Then follow the trail in reverse," Boyd said. "Research this man. Look for correlations in *his* life and the date of the murder."

"Good idea."

"You might even try checking that license number through the Texas Department of Motor Vehicles. See who the automobile's registered owner was back then."

"Thank you, professor," Charlie said, shaking hands. He started through the door, and then stopped. "If I am in town Tuesday, I will take those tests."

Boyd's smile was genuine. "Please let me know."

Charlie turned his blue Mercedes onto Wilshire Boulevard and headed east. "How am I going to prove Harlow killed Moreno?" he asked himself. He wished his name were Philip Marlowe or Sam Spade, as he mulled the professor's suggestion: "Follow the trail in reverse."

He recalled the article he'd read on Harlow in the *Times*. According to that piece, the candidate for governor was a prominent Los Angeles building contractor and civic leader. He was on one of the mayor's urban renewal committees and he was an active fund-raiser for such charities as the Arthritis Foundation and City of Hope. He was also one of the city's most eligible bachelors.

Harlow hadn't come to California until the late 1970s. Originally, he was from a little town in Texas called Muni.

"I guess I'm goin' back to Texas," Charlie said.

Just past Santa Monica Boulevard, he turned off Wilshire and into a parking lot. "I'm just going to make a couple of calls," he said, handing the attendant three dollars and heading for the pay phone by the alley.

"Where the hell is Muni, Texas?" Charlie asked the Delta reservations clerk.

"Let me check for you, sir." Charlie could hear her playing with her computer keyboard. "It's down on the Brazos River," she said after a couple of minutes. "They don't have an airport, so you'd have to fly into Dallas and rent a car."

"Can you get me on a flight early tomorrow morning?" he asked, thinking of Jenny.

The clerk fiddled with her keyboard again. "Would six-thirty be too early?"

Charlie's second call was to Paul Di Mico, who worked in the editing department of Warner Brothers Pictures. Di Mico sounded on edge. "Why are you calling me *here*?" he said.

"Don't worry," Charlie assured him. "I'm at a pay phone."

"I'm *not*"

"I wanted to talk to you before you left the studio. I'm going back to Dallas first thing tomorrow. I thought you could let me take something along to help pay for the trip."

"I got nothing for you, Charlie."

"What about the new Scorsese picture? My man would pay top dollar for that one."

83

     "Even if it *was* ready, which it's not, things are just too hot right now. After that last jaunt of yours, they're even counting the rolls of toilet paper in the heads."

     "I'll give you three big ones for it."

     "*Fuck off, Powers*!" Di Mico's voice dropped to whisper, as if somebody had come into the room. "I like workin' at the studio," he said. "I like not bein' in jail."

     "Paul, don't worry about a...." Charlie stopped talking. He realized that Di Mico had hung up.

CHAPTER EIGHT

The flight from Los Angeles landed at DFW right on schedule. Charlie, wearing jeans and his favorite polo shirt, was the first one off the plane. He went right to the Hertz rental desk where he picked up the keys to a Ford Thunderbird.

"How long do you plan to keep the car, sir?" the clerk asked him.

"I'm not sure," he said. "Maybe two or three days." Stuffing the paperwork into his attaché case, he started toward the car pick-up area.

"*Damn it!*" He was halfway there when he realized that he'd forgotten to claim his suitcase. On his previous trips to Dallas, he hadn't brought a suitcase, since he'd always arrived in the morning, completed his clandestine business, and then flown out the same afternoon. Charlie smiled at his own stupidity. He did an about face and headed for the baggage claim area.

Thirty minutes later, he was speeding along U.S. 77, pointed south. The long flat plains ahead of him appeared endless. He was looking at almost a two hundred mile drive, and he figured that, with luck, he could make Muni in about three hours. With even more good fortune, he could finish his research there and be back in Dallas by late that evening.

"Jenny will sure be surprised to see me," he said to himself. He wondered if he should call first, rather than just materialize on her doorstep at eleven at night. "What if I catch her with some other guy?" He decided to mull that decision for awhile.

—

85

He heard the beep of a horn to his right. A comely blonde with frizzy hair had pulled up alongside in her red Corvette and was giving him the once over. He recalled that's how he'd met Brenda almost two years ago.

They'd been stopped next to each other at a Sunset Strip traffic signal. She'd smiled at him. He'd smiled back. She'd turned away and looked back at the light. "Are you one of *those*?" he'd asked her.

"One of *what*?"

"One of those ladies that smiles, taunts my heart, then disappears into the traffic up ahead forever?"

She'd laughed. "That's a great line."

"Is it?" he'd smiled. "I just made it up."

Fifteen minutes later, they were having drinks together at Hamburger Hamlet. An hour after that, they drove over to the Polo Lounge in the Beverly Hills Hotel for dinner. They'd made love that night until four in the morning.

The blonde tooted her horn again, and then zoomed off down the highway. "There she goes," Charlie quipped to himself, "taunting my heart."

The memory of those good moments with Brenda saddened him. There'd been so few of them during the past few months. Her spirit of fun, of adventure seemed to have disappeared. "I want more than this," she'd said to him the night she'd suggested they live together on a regular basis. "We either have a commitment or we don't"

"There's nobody else," he'd told her truthfully. "I'm just not interested in a permanent arrangement right now."

After that incident, she seemed to withdraw. She became more career oriented, rather than "Charlie oriented." That had been okay with him. It gave him space. And, she still went with him on his business trips...for her usual twenty-five percent of the take. Up until the other night, sex had still been pretty damn good, too. But, on the other hand, she'd also become "bitchy"...more critical of him and his ideas.

Only last night, he'd been in the bedroom packing when she'd called him into the living room with a sarcastic, "Hey, your friend Harlow's on the ten o'clock news."

The television camera crew had covered the candidate's visit to a Salinas bean field. With the off-screen reporter supplying comment, they'd followed him as he sought votes from the farm workers, most of whom appeared to be of Spanish descent. A smiling Harlow, dressed in a light suit, walked up and down the rows of bean plants, shaking hands and chatting with several dozen of the people.

"He's got a nice smile," Brenda had said, "but his eyes are cold."

The TV image then cut to Harlow, now holding his jacket over his shoulder, addressing the group from a small platform. "When my opponent was campaigning four years ago," he proclaimed, "he made lots of nice promises to the farm worker. Then, he got elected." The candidate waited a beat and smirked. "I doubt if he's even *seen* a farm since."

"I can still hear a bit of the Texas," Charlie said, "can't you?" Brenda had kept studying the set and didn't answer.

"Well," Harlow continued, "I think my opponent made some pretty good promises back then, and, if you give me his job this election, I'm gonna keep *his* promises for him."

The news story had concluded with the reporter's off-camera announcement that, according to polls released that morning, Harlow had narrowed the gap to within six percentage points of incumbent Governor Stanton.

"Way to go, Bobby," Charlie said. "He's a smooth one, isn't he?"

"He's dangerous." Brenda had turned off the TV. "Count me out of this one. Blackmail's not my game."

"Who said anything about blackmail?"

"What, then, are you planning?" Her tone was snide.

The question had caught him by surprise. He'd responded with the first thing that came to mind. "I'm curious. I want to see where the trail leads." Her face remained expressionless. "Although," he'd proceeded, "it *would* be 'fun' if Harlow and I became 'buddies.' I never had a governor for a 'buddy' before."

Brenda wasn't amused. She'd gotten up from the sofa and headed for the kitchen. Still trying to unlock her sense of humor, Charlie followed. "On the other hand," he'd ad-libbed, "maybe I'll write a book...a best seller. *I Went OBE for the F.B.I.*" He'd laughed at his joke. She didn't. "Or, try this: *The Joy of OBE*."

That one had got to her. "It's too dangerous," she'd said, cracking a smile, which quickly evaporated. "If you're wrong, you're gonna face a libel suit...and, if you're right...." She'd hesitated and opened the refrigerator.

"What?"

"You're liable to be dead."

Again, he'd responded with the first thing that'd come to mind. "*Bullshit!*"

The road sign up ahead told Charlie that he was twenty-five miles outside of Waco. According to the map on the seat next to him, that's where he had to swing southeast onto Highway 6, which ran parallel to the Brazos.

He decided that the thing that was *really* upsetting about the way Brenda talked to him was that it was starting to remind him of the way that his mother used to talk to his father. When she'd had a few drinks in her, which was often, the bloated woman spat words that could turn the most macho of men into a eunuch.

"Why do you want to run this cruddy pawnshop?" she'd spew at her wiry husband at least once a week. "Why don't we open up a *nice* jewelry store up on Fifth Avenue?"

"I like working on the street," he'd answer without looking at her.

"You like working with bums? With drunks?"

Charlie would almost feel sick watching his father shrink under her onslaught. "Please, Evelyn," the older man would virtually beg as he straightened some watches in the showcase, "just let me be."

"Let me be. Let me be," she'd mimic. "Do you know how much it embarrasses me to even come *in* here?"

"*Stop it, mom!*" Charlie had been nineteen that one time he'd taken his father's part. "Leave him alone."

"Are you turning against me, too?" she'd snapped.

"No....Just stop picking on him."

She'd stood there fuming for a few moments, and then turned on her heel and stormed out of the store. "Son, you'd better go after her," his father had said. "Maybe *you* can calm her down."

—

89

Charlie couldn't understand how his father could be so forgiving. "What about you?" he'd asked, recalling that two local shopkeepers had been robbed earlier that week.

"I'll be fine."

"You want to lock the door behind me?"

His father had smiled and shrugged in that special warm way that was all his own. "Then how would the customers get in?" he'd said. "Now, go get your mother before she gets herself into trouble."

"Okay."

"Tonight, on the way home, we'll stop by the video store, his father had said. They're holding *Command Decision* with Clark Gable for us. You'll like that movie."

As Charlie had stepped out into the nippy Seattle air, he'd almost collided with Tommy, a wino who always seemed to be wearing the same buttoned-up soiled overcoat. His father had ordered the belligerent forty-year-old out of the store on several occasions. The most recent time was just two days earlier, when Tommy had decided to urinate on one of the showcases.

"Watch where you're goin', *asshole*!" Tommy growled as Charlie had pushed by him.

Charlie ignored the man. He took a few steps up First and spotted his mother at the corner, trying to hail a taxi. "Mom," he'd said as he hurried up to her, "come back to the store."

"Don't you touch me!" She'd pulled away from him and stepped out into the street. "*Taxi!*" she'd shouted at the cab that sped past her.

Charlie was both frightened and amused by her anger. "Mom, you're gonna get hit!"

"I'd be better off." Tears had started to form in her
eyes. "Nobody gives a damn about me anyway."

She was playing the "Pity Mother" game again.
Charlie had been forced to play it with her ever since he
was a little kid. She'd begin by drowning herself in scotch,
and then she'd bemoan the fact that she'd "married beneath
herself." Next, she'd look at her only child and ask, "Do
you love Mommy?"

Charlie had learned early that an affirmative
answer and a big hug could bring him a candy bar, a comic
book, a ticket to the local movie theater or, as he grew
older, a few extra dollars in his pocket.

But, the game had become tired. It wasn't a game
anymore. It hadn't been for some time.

"I give a damn, Mom," Charlie had said with
manufactured emotion, escorting her back onto the
sidewalk. He hugged her without affection.

She wiped her tears. "Then, why do you protect
him?"

"He *is* my father. I can love him, too, you know."

"If he really cared for his family," she'd said, "he'd
open up a nice store. Something elegant...."

Charlie had interrupted her. "He wouldn't be
happy on Fifth Avenue." He shot a glance in the direction
of the store. Some people were gathered out front. "I've
got to get back," he said, suddenly concerned.

Charlie made the turn onto Highway 6. He
checked the map again and calculated that the Muni turn-
off should be coming up in about twenty minutes.

He drifted back into his memory and that night
he'd hurried back down the block to the pawnshop. He'd

pushed his way through the anxious crowd outside. Tommy and Mr. Weiss, the old gent who ran the tailor shop next door, were looking at something lying on the floor near a back showcase. A man that Charlie didn't know was behind the counter, talking on the telephone. "Send an ambulance," the man had said. "I think it's a heart attack."

Charlie felt his legs go numb. He stopped in the middle of the store. He didn't have to see his father. He knew he was dead.

"What's the matter? Is something wrong?" His mother's hysterical voice sliced through the babbling of the crowd that was threatening to overflow into the store. It brought Charlie back to reality. Tear ducts opened wide, she'd rushed over to him and grasped his shoulders. "What's happened to your father?"

He'd turned and looked her in the eye. "You finally killed him. Satisfied?"

Charlie had left her standing there alone to play the grieving widow. By the time she'd reached home that night, he had packed and left. He moved in with a friend at college.

For appearances sake, he did stand by his mother at the funeral. And, for a fee of ten thousand dollars, he even helped her to close up the store and liquidate the stock. But, they never really spoke again. There were no conversations. No hugs.

At the end of the semester, he'd left school. He took his ten grand and moved to Los Angeles.

He never saw his mother again. He'd heard she'd died of cancer of the liver about three years ago.

Some nights when he was alone, Charlie still cried for his father.

The sign where Charlie turned off the main highway read: "Muni, 3 miles. Visit Our Museum of the Old West." The arrow pointed to a blacktopped road that appeared to lead off into nowhere.

"Who the hell would want to visit a museum all the way out here?" Charlie asked himself.

His gut answered back. "Run! Get the hell out of here!"

He hesitated for a minute. "Maybe it's just hungry," he reasoned, as he turned south and headed down the ill-kept road.

CHAPTER NINE

"I don't believe this," Charlie said to himself.

His initial impulse upon seeing the town of Muni
was to crack a variation of the old joke: "I'd better not
blink as I drive through, or I'll miss it."

Then, he felt that now familiar chill pass through
his body again. He took a nibble on his fingernail, and
began to wonder if he wasn't having, as Matt in the
hospital would've put it, "another 'Twilight Zone' type of
experience." Except this time, instead of traveling out of
body, he was traveling into the fantasy of one of his
favorite movies. He knew exactly how Spencer Tracy
must have felt when he stepped off of that train in *Bad
Day at Black Rock*, unimpressed, disbelieving and,
perhaps a bit anxious.

Muni was Black Rock brought to life. All that
was missing was the railroad station.

On one side of the blacktopped road were three
small wooden houses with cracked windows, peeling
white paint and front yards boasting gardens of sagebrush
and overgrown weeds. That was Muni's residential
section.

Across the road were the commercial and
industrial areas. The commercial element entailed three
buildings, built early in the 20th century and connected by
a wooden sidewalk.

The industrial side had even more character. It consisted of a large empty corral, complete with several piles of dried horse dung, and a service station.

"GAS" was the only message on the station's signpost, but a huge red star was leaning against the side of the cracked stucco building and smaller insignia were still affixed to the out-of-date pumps.

Charlie wondered how long it had been since Texaco had pulled their franchise.

He stopped at one of the two pumps and honked his horn. The attendant didn't appear to be about, although the door to the station was open and an old Chevy pick-up was parked by the side of the structure.

"Shit!" Charlie wanted to stay in the car. He could see the heat rising from the road, and he didn't much feel like leaving the comfort of his air-conditioned vehicle to go looking for some local yokel to pump gas for him.

He honked again, then looked at his watch. It was four o'clock. He was going to have to get moving if he hoped to finish in Muni before it got too late.

"Anybody around?" he shouted, as he emerged from the Thunderbird. He received no answer. His polo shirt had already begun to adhere itself to his perspiring torso. He pulled at it, as he walked around the side of the building and got his first good look of Muni's commercial district.

"They've undergone rural renewal," he quipped, noting that the three ancient wooden structures appeared to have been painted within the past five years.

The buildings included the two-storey Muni House hotel, including cafe and bar, Billy's General Store, and a combination real estate, insurance and notary public office. The sign on that building also read "Office of the Mayor."

"Big City Politics," Charlie muttered to himself. He wondered where all the people were. He wondered where *anybody* was.

There was a fourth, much newer, wooden structure. Freshly painted and well kept, it was detached from the others and situated near the roadside. The hand-carved placard above it read "Old West Museum". Nobody was around there either.

"It's a regular boom town," Charlie said, as he headed back to his car. He honked his horn a couple more times.

"Hold on, mister. I'm a comin'." The gangling station attendant rushed around from the side of the building, zipping up his fly.

"Fill 'er up," Charlie said. He wondered how long it had been since the guy had washed his uniform, or if he'd ever washed it.

The attendant jammed the gas nozzle into the Thunderbird. "I'm here all alone, you know," he said, squeezing the puss out of a pimple on his face. "I can't piss and pump gas at the same time."

Charlie flashed his "charming, casual conversation" smile. "You live here long?"

"All my life."

"Really?" Charlie figured the guy to be in his early forties, but under all that grime it was hard to tell.

"This station used to be my daddy's 'fore he died."

"I guess you're planning to pass it down through the generations," Charlie quipped to himself.

"Huh?" The attendant's confused smile revealed a mouth of misdirected teeth.

Charlie figured he'd better control his sense of humor in Muni. "Then you must've known Bob Harlow."

The man stopped pumping the gas. He stopped smiling, too. "What for you wanna know that?" he asked.

"Proceed with care," Charlie reasoned. "I write for a newspaper," he said. "We're doing a story on him."

"You're gonna have to talk to Mr. Mason."

"Who's that?"

"He's our mayor and justice o' peace." He turned away from Charlie and began to pump gas again. "He said that anybody that comes around askin' 'bout Mr. Harlow should be sent right to him."

Charlie could see he wasn't going to get anything else from this guy. "Where do I find Mr. Mason?"

"He owns the insurance office over there," the attendant said, pointing toward the commercial buildings.

"Okay if I leave my car here?"

The man still didn't look at him. "I'll park 'er in the shade."

"Thanks." Charlie trudged over toward the buildings. Halfway there, he had to stop to pull a thorn out of his sock and dump a pebble from his shoe. He mounted the wooden steps and entered the "Office of the Mayor."

"Can I help you, son?" The big beefy man was seated behind the wooden railing, his feet propped up on a roll-top desk. Charlie took him to be about sixty-five. He thought that the tailored western suit he was wearing made him look like a caricature of that cowboy caricature that had once sold cars on television back in Los Angeles.

"Are you Mr. Mason?"

"Crock Mason. That's me." The man put down his newspaper and flashed *his* charming smile. Charlie had a notion that the two of them could compete against each other in the "Smile of the Month" contest.

"I'm with the *San Diego Union*," Charlie said. "We're doing a profile on Bob Harlow."

His eyes made a quick survey of the one room office. Its decor was mostly "Old West", punctuated with a couple of large Remington prints on the walls and a functional, if out-of-place, ceiling fan that looked like it had been stolen from the set of *Casablanca*.

Across the way from Mason, a homemade placard, reading "Insurance is Your Best Investment" hung over a small wooden desk. A skinny woman with a ponytail occupied the desk. She was working at a typewriter almost as old as her. Charlie figured that she had to be about forty-five, but under all that foundation and rouge, he was taking a ten-year handicap either way.

"You come to the right place," Mason drawled, standing up and extending his hand. "We're pretty proud of Bobby here."

"I'll bet you are."

"What was your handle?"

Charlie gave the man one of the business cards he'd had printed up for such an occasion. "I'm Al Parsons," he said.

Mason studied the card, and then exuding that insincere hospitality that Charlie knew could only be found in Texas or Los Angeles, he handed it to his secretary. "Alice, honey," he said, "this here's Mr. Al Parsons of the *San Diego Union* Newspaper."

Charlie couldn't help thinking that an unspoken message had been passed between them. His gut spoke-up again: "Get the hell out of here, asshole!"

"What can I do for you, Mr. Parsons?" Mason asked.

"I was hoping you could give me some background information. You know, what was Harlow like when he lived here? That sort of thing."

Mason grabbed his wide-brimmed hat from the desk and stepped through the gate. "He were a hard workin' boy," he said. "He liked to build things. He built a new room on my folks' place...all by his self."

"Sounds enterprising."

"Oh, he was." Mason opened the office door. "Come on. I want to show you something." As Charlie preceded him out, the older man turned back to the secretary. "You make that call, now," he said.

"Right away." She picked up the phone and began to dial.

"When did Bobby leave Muni?" Charlie asked, as he followed Mason down the sidewalk toward the road. He was in awe at how unaffected the man was by the heat.

"That were back in the mid-seventies sometime. He moved up to Dallas. There were more opportunities there. He got in the construction business. Even took some of them night school courses, I understand." Mason waved to a gray-haired gent in the hotel lobby. "But, every few months Bobby'd come home for a visit," he continued. "He never forgot us."

They stepped off the sidewalk and headed over to the town's newest structure. "He gave us the money to build this here museum," Mason said. We needed *somethin'* to put our town on the map. We don't got no Alamo here, you know."

The museum door was unlocked. Mason switched on the lights and invited Charlie to enter. "There's some interesting things here," he said with pride.

Charlie looked around the paneled one-room gallery, which appeared to be a thrown together set-up of display cases, filled with western memorabilia, and wall posters. From its position on the center wall, a large one-sheet of John Wayne from *Red River* dominated the room.

Mason beckoned his guest over to one of the display cases. "This here's a pair o' Sam Houston's boots," he said. "And that gun over there once belonged to John Wesley Hardin."

Viewing the exhibits, Charlie couldn't help wondering if those scuffed-up boots and that rusted six-shooter were authentic, or just some things that Mason had lying around his house. "This is fascinating," he said, forcing himself to sound interested. "Where'd you get all this...'stuff'?" He congratulated himself for switching nouns at the last second.

"Here and there. I designed the whole set-up myself."

"I can tell," Charlie murmured.

"What was that?"

Charlie beamed the "charming smile" again. "I was just thinking," he said, "that this is amazing. I've never seen anything like this in my life."

Mason seemed pleased. "Thank you, son," he said.

The older man began to worry Charlie. He couldn't believe that he was that stupid.

"We get tourists, now," Mason said, as they walked back to his office. "Not a lot. But, come summer, two or three cars a day drive through. Folks want to see a real Texas cow town."

"I don't see any cows," Charlie observed. "Don't see any horses, either."

"Son," Mason laughed, "these days, cowboys don't ride horses much. They mostly ride around in jeeps and pick-ups." He waved again to the old gent in the hotel. "Come tonight though, the boys'll drift in off the local ranches to have a few beers. Week-ends, they drive into Waco."

"I see."

Mason turned to face Charlie. "Everything we got here in Muni we owe to Bobby Harlow," he said. "He financed the museum. He paid to restore the hotel and these other buildings, too. An', when he gets 'lected governor o' California, we're *really* gonna have somethin' to brag about."

"I'm sure you will," Charlie nodded. "How'd Bobby wind up in California anyway?"

"I don't rightly know. Some business opportunity, I reckon."

"He moved there in the late seventies, didn't he?"

"'Bout then," Mason answered, entering his office. "He sorta left without much advance notice. We just got a card from 'im one day...." He hesitated a moment to read a note his secretary had handed him.

Charlie didn't like the way the woman seemed to avoid looking at him. He chalked it up to paranoia and began to ask another question. "Do you know who...?"

"Mr. Parsons," Mason interrupted, "how'd you like to talk with Bobby's cousin?"

The offer surprised Charlie. "Sure."

"He can help with the more personal stuff better than me."

"Where do I find him?"

"Pete runs the Harlow family ranch these days," Mason said. He picked up a scratch pad and started to rough out a map. "It's about five miles south o' town...right on the river."

"I just follow the road out here around?" Charlie asked.

"That's right. I'll call ahead an' let 'im know you're coming."

Walking back to his car, Charlie kept mulling over his conversation with Mason. He couldn't help wondering who'd conned who.

CHAPTER TEN

The secretary bothered him.

He didn't like the way she'd acted when he'd come back into the office with Mason, and he didn't figure her to be the shy type.

"It was almost as if she knew some secret," Charlie said to himself, "and she was afraid that, if she looked at me, I'd know it, too."

He braked for a jack rabbit that scampered across the dirt road, then watched it zig-zag down toward the river. Up ahead, he could see a half-dozen cattle grazing in a large section of fenced rangeland. The sign on the end post read: "Harlow Ranch, No Trespassing".

"Could she have called San Diego to check me out?" Charlie remembered the way he'd sensed that Mason was giving his secretary an unspoken message when he'd handed her his phony business card. "Big deal!" he rationalized. "If they find out there's no Al Parsons, I can always say I work part time. What do they call it?...A 'stringer'."

He told his gut to shut up.

Without slowing, Charlie hung a wide right and passed through the wooden archway with the name "Harlow" painted across its top. Another three-dozen or so cattle, plus a roan and her colt, were grazing behind barbed wire fencing that ran along the left side of the dusty access road. He was driving west, and with the sun's rays reflecting off the river, he had to squint to get a glimpse of the ranch house up ahead.

The Thunderbird bounced over a bump, as it entered the ranch yard. A flock of chickens, led by a large goose, scurried out of the vehicle's path. Charlie parked over by the empty corral and got out.

The place did not meet his expectations. It wasn't the Southfork from the old "Dallas" TV show, nor was it even the Reata from George Stevens' *Giant*. More than anything, Harlow's ranch reminded Charlie of Ma and Pa Kettle's farm.

The ranch-style house, its yellow color faded from years of windstorms, was in only slightly better repair than those homes he'd seen in town. Two broken windowpanes had been patched with cardboard and the discarded screen door was leaning against the outside wall. A metal porch swing in need of oiling creaked, as it swayed back-and-forth by the light river breeze that had brought a large tumbleweed up to rest in front of the door.

Aside from the gathering of fowl, Charlie didn't see much sign of life on the place. "Anybody here?" he shouted, spotting an almost new Ford pick-up parked next to the barn. He noted that the once gray building needed its left door put back onto its hinges.

"Yeah!" The gruff voice came from inside the barn.

Charlie tasted his fingernail. He did not relish the prospect of entering the dark byre. "Al Parsons," he called. "Mr. Mason was supposed to have phoned about me."

"He phoned." The man stepped out of the barn carrying a large hammer and a box of nails. He was

dressed in overalls and a T-shirt, and wore a straw Stetson.
He was also wearing a scowl.

"Oh, shit!" Charlie muttered, wondering what
Mason had told the man. The last time he'd remembered
seeing anyone that massive was Lon Chaney, Jr.'s
"Lennie" in the old classic movie, *Of Mice and Men*.
"Hey, George," he attempted joking to himself, "tell me
about the rabbits."

Gripping the hammer, the man started across the
yard toward him. Charlie judged that he was pushing
sixty. Certainly he could outrun the guy, if that became
necessary. He considered a retreat to the relative safety of
the Thunderbird.

"Hello," the man said, extending his hand and
beaming a warm smile, "I'm Pete Harlow."

"Al Parsons." Charlie hoped his sigh of relief
wasn't too obvious.

"Crock Mason said you'd be comin' right out."

"You live here alone?"

"Since my wife died." Pete stuck the hammer into
his pocket and pointed to his truck. "Come take a ride
with me," he said. "I got a chore to do."

"It's a big place for one man to run," Charlie said.
He climbed into the vehicle and saw that a twelve-gauge
shotgun was resting in a mount above the windshield.

"I get help when I need it." Pete started the motor
and directed the truck to a narrow dirt road that ran behind
the barn down toward the river. Charlie braced himself, as
it bounced over a series of rocks and chuckholes.

"Do you operate the ranch for your cousin?" he
asked.

"Bobby and me are partners."

"How often docs hc gct down here?"

"Not often."

Charlie could see that, unlike Mason, Pete was not the talkative type. He decided not to rush things. "Where are we going?"

Pete slowed to let a steer cross the road. "Gotta mend a fence," he said. "Calf got stuck in quicksand this mornin'." He pulled over to where a fifty-foot section of the riverbank had been fenced off with barbed wire. A crudely lettered sign read: "Danger, Quicksand." Two of the posts had been knocked down, allowing entry to a large muddy area that ran down to the water.

The large man walked over to one of the posts and began to right it. "Need any help?" Charlie asked, following him.

"I can handle it." Pete pushed the post to its upright position.

Charlie strolled over to the edge of the fence. "There much quicksand around here?" he asked.

"A few spots along the river." He pounded the post back into its hole. "You know much about quicksand, Mr. Parsons?"

"Just what I've seen in the movies."

"It's dangerous stuff," Pete said. He finished with the one post and sauntered over in Charlie's direction. "A man could step into a pool like this, an' in a minute, he'd disappear forever. Nobody'd ever know what became of him."

"I imagine it holds a lot of secrets," Charlie replied, unconcerned that Pete was standing directly behind him.

"It sure does."

Charlie felt Pete's huge left paw grasp him at the scruff of the neck. The other hand took hold of the seat of his pants. Before he realized what had happened, he was off his feet, being propelled up and outward toward the pool of quicksand. "*Hey!*" he shouted.

He landed on his stomach. "Christ, man," he said, his voice betraying his horror, "what are you doing!?!" The panic set in, as his legs began to sink beneath the surface. He tried to right himself, moving his arms in a wild attempt to row himself back toward the solid ground.

"Don't struggle," Pete said with amusement. "You'll sink faster that way."

Charlie felt the ooze close in around his waist. His eyes darted in every direction, looking for a way out.

Pete spit out into the pool. "You think we're a bunch o' dumb assholes here, don't ya, boy?" he said. "You figured you could put one over on us."

"What are you talking about!?!" Charlie screamed. "Help me!"

"Ol' Crock, he called yer paper in San Diego," Pete said, picking his teeth with a grimy finger. "They never heard of you."

"I'm a free lancer." Charlie shouted out his prepared answer, knowing it would have no effect on the man.

"Bullshit!" Pete called. He strolled back to the pick-up. "You write fer one of them...scandal papers, I'll bet."

The mud had reached Charlie's lower ribs. He was feeling again like the small child who used to lie awake in the dark, frightened of the imaginary monsters of the night.

"We've had yer kind here before," Pete continued. "All you want to do is write somethin' bad about Bobby."

———

107

"No," Charlie said, tears forming in his eyes. "That's wrong."

Pete took a long coil of rope from the back of the pick-up and waved it for Charlie to see. "You tell the truth, now."

Charlie's mind raced through his limited options. He knew he couldn't tell the truth. That would put him in more trouble than he was in now...*if* that was possible. He decided to give his tormentor the answer he was looking for. "Okay!" he cried. "I freelance for *The Globe*."

"An' what're you doin' down here?" What're you after?"

"Nothin'."

Pete waved the rope again and grinned.

"This is a 'fishing expedition'," Charlie said. "I swear." Detecting no reaction from Pete, he added, "I got a wife and kids at home." He stared at the man with the sincerest expression he could muster.

Pete studied him for a few seconds. "Then, come on out," he said finally, tossing the rope back into the truck.

Charlie froze momentarily. He was unable to comprehend the man's cruelty. "Please, help me," he sobbed, losing total control of both his emotions and his bladder. "There's no story here. I'll leave town."

He saw that Pete was laughing at him, and wondered what it was like to drown in quicksand. He prayed it didn't hurt. "Don't let me die," he said softly.

"I said to come on out, boy." Pete was truly enjoying the moment.

His words didn't register with Charlie.

"That ain't quicksand," he continued. "That's a four-foot deep mud hole."

Charlie realized that he had stopped sinking. His feet were resting on the solid bottom.

"You city boys just don't know the difference, do you?"

Charlie's initial flush of relief began to turn to anger, as Harlow's laughter grated on his ears. He wasn't used to playing the victim. He didn't like the role, especially when he'd made such an emotional jerk of himself. "You fucking bastard!" he shouted, as he started to wade slowly out of the goo.

"Just take 'er easy, boy." Pete reached into the cab of the pick-up and brought out the twelve-gauge. "We're goin' back to my place an' do some more talkin'." He pumped a shell into the chamber. "After that, *if* you're lucky, I'll kick your ass outta town."

Covered with mud, Charlie reached the edge of the pool and collapsed onto the ground. He couldn't remember when in his life he'd wanted to kill somebody more than Pete. He also knew that he might forgive the man and even kiss his ass if he'd just let him take a shower.

"Toss yer wallet this way," Pete said.

"Fuck you!"

The blast from the shotgun fired into the air made Charlie jump. He found the wallet in his back pocket and threw it to Harlow. "'Charles Powers from Los Angeles'," the big man read aloud. "Hell, you even lied about your name." He pocketed the soaked currency and tossed the wallet back to Charlie. "Get in the back o' the truck," he ordered.

Charlie didn't feel like getting up yet. He was so drained that he might never want to get up again. Pete pumped another shell into the chamber. "Move!" he said.

Charlie scrambled to his feet, and then trudged over to the pick-up. Even the act of walking was a physical chore, and Pete, the weapon cradled in his arms, seemed to be relishing his plight. He wished that he were James Bond, or even Jason Bourne. They'd be out of this mess by now.

Seeing that he didn't have the energy to boost himself into the rear of the pick-up, Pete grabbed Charlie by the seat of the pants and tossed him in. He landed on top of some old pieces of lumber. "Damn it!" Charlie shouted. "Leave me alone!"

Harlow grabbed the rope from the truck and made ready to tie down his prisoner. "Hell, you ain't goin' nowhere," he decided, viewing the prone figure. He threw the rope back into the truck, and then climbed into the cab. Once more, he guffawed, as he mimicked Charlie's plea, "Don't let me die!"

The first bump almost bounced Charlie out of the pick-up. The next one caused him to hit his head against the back of the cab. "Fucking son-of-a-bitch!" he muttered, grabbing hold of the side panel. The mud had started to cake on his face, and he was having difficulty with his vision. He could hear Pete laughing, as the man seemed to deliberately hit every hole and bump in the road.

The possibility of his imminent death was no longer of prime concern to Charlie. There was only one thing he wanted. He wanted to get that fucker.

A cow and her calf crossed the road, causing Pete to stop. Charlie took the opportunity to snatch up an old soiled blanket that was lying next to him. He wiped some of the mud off his face, and then as he discarded the rag, he spotted a couple of 2x4s next to the coil of rope. One of them was about three feet long.

Pete wheeled the pick-up into the ranch yard, scattering the chickens and their goose leader. He parked next to the Thunderbird and started to climb out of the cab. The shotgun was in his right hand.

Charlie brought down the 2x4 just as his head cleared the cab. The blow caught Pete on the back of the neck. He stumbled, but did not fall. His grip tightened, discharging the weapon into the fowl.

Before the large man could recover, Charlie had leaped from the back of the truck and used the board to ram him in the kidney. A third blow landed on the top of Pete's skull. "Fall, you overgrown son-of-a-bitch!" he yelled.

Still on his feet, Pete turned to face his attacker. He raised the shotgun like a club. Charlie smashed him again, this time across the left side of the head. The board broke, leaving Charlie holding about a foot of splintered wood.

Pete was bleeding from below the eye, but still standing. He made ready to swing the shotgun. "I'm gonna kill ya, cocksucker!" he growled.

Charlie thrust forward, stabbing Pete's face with the needle-sharp splinters. The man screamed and dropped the shotgun.

Charlie made a dive for the weapon, but Pete brought up his right fist and caught him in the gut. Charlie doubled over. Fighting for his breath, he collapsed to his knees.

Pete yanked the stub of 2x4 out of his bleeding cheek and flung it into the dirt. He pulled Charlie to his feet, slamming him into the side of the truck.

A sharp pain shot down Charlie's spine. He saw Pete pull back his fist to deliver what he knew would be the "death blow." He also saw the shotgun lying on the ground...about six feet away. He knew that was his only chance.

He brought up his knee hard and caught Pete in the crotch. The big man screamed and doubled over.

Charlie made a dive for the shotgun. He grabbed it and scrambled to his feet, pumping a fresh shell into the chamber.

Still nursing his pain, Pete started to back away.

Charlie screamed at him. "Sit down, Pete, *you shithead*!!"

Harlow hesitated. Charlie pointed the gun at his crotch. "Sit down, or I'll blast it off," he said.

Pete plopped down next to the pick-up.

"Nice truck you got there," Charlie said. He leveled the gun at the vehicle and pulled the trigger. The blast disintegrated the left front tire. He pumped another shell into the chamber and pointed it at Pete.

Harlow blanched. His mouth hung agape.

For an instant, Charlie seriously considered pulling the trigger on this bastard that had shamed and degraded him. Then, he remembered why he was there.

"Now," he said, "if you don't want to wind up like that dead goose over there, we're going to have a nice little interview."

Charlie killed his headlights about a quarter mile outside of Muni. Thankful for the full moon, he crept the Thunderbird along the dirt road until he was just at the outskirts of the town. He turned off the motor and waited.

The only lights in Muni were coming from the saloon portion of the hotel. Three or four drunken voices, Crock Mason's among them, carried over the distance, as did a jukebox recording of an old Hank Williams tune. As far as Charlie could tell, there was nobody down by the service station or the museum.

Charlie wondered if he'd tied Pete securely enough to that post in the barn. He was a strong man. He might be able to break loose without a hell of a lot of trouble. And, once he did, he'd be on a horse and on his way to town. Disabling his truck and his telephone wasn't going to dissuade a guy like Pete.

Charlie studied the structure of the museum, and tried to figure the best way to pull off the plan he'd formulated while driving the last five miles. The place was really not much more than wood siding, nailed to a simple frame. "Beautiful." Charlie said to himself, contemplating what might be the building's weakest point.

Inside the hotel's saloon, a woman laughed.

Charlie saw two people emerge from the saloon. It was Mason and his secretary. He had his arm around her waist. "The cocksucker's gonna get laid," Charlie mused, happy to have an audience.

He turned the key in the ignition and gunned the motor. Then, he drove slowly past the museum, so that Mason could see him.

From the hotel porch, the Texan looked at Charlie with a combination of surprise and smug amusement. "G'bye, Mr. Parsons," he called with a wave. "Good riddance."

Again, Charlie gunned his motor. He backed up the Thunderbird, and then pressed down on the gas pedal, racing toward the far end of town.

Mason was confused. He had no idea what "this nut" was doing, until he saw him make a wide U-turn and tear back toward the museum. "*No...*," he squealed, his expression turning to one of horror.

The Thunderbird smashed into the east wall of the fragile structure and kept on moving. Splinters flew everywhere. The roof began to sag. As the vehicle emerged through the other side, it took with it the last remaining supports. The building collapsed into a pile of firewood.

Charlie spun the car around to face Mason, who appeared frozen to the porch. "How's that, Crock?" he called, extending his middle finger. "Now, we're even."

Mason exploded. He started down the three wooden steps toward Charlie, and stumbled. He landed on his face. His secretary rushed to help him to his feet.

"*I'll kill him!*" Charlie heard the older man shout. He headed the Thunderbird back toward the main highway.

Crocker Mason turned and looked at what was once his museum... his dream come true.

Crocker Mason wept.

CHAPTER ELEVEN

Charlie awoke at ten the next morning, painfully aware of every bone and muscle in his body. The note on the pillow next to him read, "Gone to work. Walk Roger. See you later. Luv, Jen."

He looked over at the corner armchair. Roger growled at him.

He'd arrived on Jenny's doorstep about eight hours earlier, looking like the perennial corpse that had been dragged out of a swamp. "Don't ask," he'd said before she could even open her mouth.

While he'd showered, then soaked for almost an hour in a tub, Jenny had thrown what remained of his clothes into the wash and made him some soup and sandwiches. He'd thought that all he wanted to do was sleep, but after he'd climbed into bed with her, he'd found that there was a good hour's worth of energy left in him yet.

Ready to meet the day, he scooted up in bed, reached for the phone and dialed. Brenda's voice sounded groggy. "I'm sorry," he said, looking at the bedside clock radio that read 9AM. "I forgot about the time difference."

"Are you okay?" she asked. "When I didn't hear from you, I got worried."

Charlie gave her a quick rundown of his harrowing experience in Muni. "Why don't you get the hell out of there, Charlie?" she snapped.

He pretended he hadn't heard her. "When Robert Harlow was nineteen," he said, summarizing what he'd learned from Pete, "he knocked up some Mexican gal. She was the daughter of a migrant worker. He's got an illegitimate kid running around someplace."

"It sounds like Muni's trying to protect the good name of their favorite son," she suggested.

"Sounds that way."

Her tone turned sarcastic. "You're lucky you weren't lynched."

"Don't laugh. I'm still in Texas."

"But, did you find out anything *useful*?"

Charlie sometimes hated the way Brenda always cut down to the bottom line of the issue. Other times, he found it quite helpful. "Harlow liked to hunt...with a shotgun," he offered.

"So do a lot of people."

"As far as the people in Muni knew, he was a plain ol' blue collar worker in Dallas, tryin' to better himself. Then, one day, he packs up and goes off to L.A. Told his cousin he'd bought a piece of land there, had gotten financing and was going to build some tract homes on it."

"Where'd he get the money?"

Charlie said. "I think he got it out of a suitcase."

"Prove it."

"Good ol' negative Brenda," he said, wishing he'd never called her.

"Listen to you!" she said. "You don't have one piece of real evidence, and you're ready to take Harlow out and shoot him." She started to yell. "Damn it! You don't even know if you dreamed the whole thing."

"You're wrong, babe," he said. "I do have a piece of evidence."

"What?"

"I got a license number."

Charlie arrived at the Department of Motor Vehicles wearing a fresh pair of jeans and a sports shirt. None of the three clerks behind the counter appeared particularly busy. He chose to approach a plump woman in her fifties, who wore wire-rimmed glasses and reminded him of his third grade teacher, Mrs. Truitt.

He'd always been able to put one over on Mrs. Truitt.

"I'd like to trace a license number," he said to the woman.

Without looking up from the form she was checking, the clerk handed him a small index card. "Fill this out, please."

It took Charlie less than a minute to complete the task. "I want to know who owned that car in May of 1978," he said.

The clerk looked up, surprised. "That's a long time ago," she said.

"You can do it, can't you?"

"Yes." She leaned her head back and regarded him with some incredulity. "Why would you want information this old?"

"It's an insurance matter."

"It'll take a few minutes," she said. He could see she was no Mrs. Truitt.

"I'll be right here." He beamed his "charming" smile at her. She didn't seem impressed, as she headed back toward the files.

"Please, God," he thought to himself, "let it be Robert Harlow."

Charlie spent the next twenty minutes perusing the office bulletin board. He read about the civil service jobs being offered, and he committed to memory the building rules. He was about to study the posted fire escape plan when he saw a familiar ruddy face over at the counter, talking to a clerk. The face had a stogie clenched in its teeth and sat atop a size 50 out-of-style suit.

"Hello, son," Mal Wiggins said. "Still workin' on your 'book'?"

"Still workin' on it," Charlie replied, wishing that Wiggins wasn't there. He didn't need an investigative crime reporter trying to find out what he was doing.

Wiggins handed a small index card to the clerk, who retreated to the files. "I gotta to find out the name of the little punk that sideswiped me last week," he said to Charlie. "He took off, but I got his license number."

"Let's hope he has insurance," Charlie said. He wished "Mrs. Truitt" would return, so that he could get out of there.

"If he doesn't have it, I'm sure his daddy does," Wiggins said. "He was drivin' a BMW."

Charlie managed another smile.

"How's your research goin'?" Wiggins asked.

"Fine."

The reporter appeared disappointed that he didn't elaborate. "I'd've thought you'd be gone by now," he pressed.

"Probably today or tomorrow." Charlie spotted "Mrs. Truitt" returning from the files. "Excuse me," he said to Wiggins, moving down the counter a few feet to get out of his earshot. The newsman drifted a step or two after him.

"I have your information," the clerk announced. Charlie wished she possessed a softer voice.

"Yes?" He turned his back to Wiggins and held his breath. "Let it be Robert Harlow," he thought. "*Please let it be Robert Harlow.*"

"In 1978," she said, reading from a slip of paper, "license number 'DYK 730' was assigned to a 1976 Ford station wagon."

"Yeah?" he grinned.

"The owner was Simon Flynn."

Charlie stopped grinning.

"Would you like his address?"

"Simon Flynn!?!...Are you sure?"

The clerk thrust the slip of paper at him. "Sir, the records don't lie."

Charlie stared at the name. He wanted it to be a mistake. "Thank you," he said, as he wandered toward the exit.

"Something wrong, son?" Wiggins asked.

"No," Charlie said, "I just...." A fresh idea caused him to stop mid-sentence. "See you around," he said, heading out the door.

"Never had a request like that before," the plump clerk said to Wiggins. "He was tracing a license number that went all the way back to 1976."

"Really?" Wiggins responded with professional curiosity. "And, who owned this car?"

"Somebody named Simon Flynn."

The reporter ran the name through his mental filing cabinet and came up empty. "Tell me," he said, "where do I find your pay phone?"

"Where's your tool box?"

The question caught Charlie with his mouth half open. He stared at the stringy, nearly bald, old geezer who'd just opened the door and momentarily wondered if God was playing "Twilight Zone" with him again. "Ah..." he stammered, "are you Simon Flynn?"

"I live here, don't I?" the man snapped. "I must be Simon Flynn. Now, where's your goddamn tool box?"

Charlie's silent smile caused Flynn to hesitate. He reached under the perspiration stained white T-shirt he was wearing and scratched his belly. "Ain't you the plumber?" he asked.

"No."

"Shit!" Flynn slammed his wooden cane against the doorframe.

"What's the problem?" Charlie asked.

"My toilet's cracked." Flynn started to shut the door. "Whole damn bathroom's flooded."

"I just need a minute of your time."

"Come back tomorrow."

"Maybe I can help." He stuck his hand out to prevent the door from closing.

"Yeah?" Flynn re-opened the door. "You think so?"

"I've fixed a john or two in my day," Charlie said, remembering the plumbing problems he'd had with his apartment down on Vermont. He knew he'd have to deal with Flynn's problem before he'd get any information out of him.

"I hope so...cause I gotta take a leak."

Flynn stepped back and let the younger man enter the small frame house. Judging from the photo of the matronly woman on the Toshiba TV, plus the newspapers and dirty dishes scattered about the living room, Charlie pegged Flynn as a retired widower.

The sole bathroom was located between the two bedrooms. Its floor was covered with water that had also seeped out to dampen the frayed carpet in the hallway. "I think it looks worse than it actually is," Charlie said after he'd inspected the commode.

"How so?" Flynn rested his weight on the cane.

Charlie pointed to a hairline crack in the bowl. "The water didn't come out of here," he said. "I think it just overflowed."

Flynn had a revelation. "I *did* drop a medicine bottle down there last night," he said. "Could that've done it?"

"Dumb old fart!" Charlie muttered to himself. "You'd better know something useful."

He found a plunger, mop and bucket buried in Flynn's kitchen utility closet. While the seventy-five-year-old man watched from a stool in the hallway, he extracted the medicine bottle from the toilet, and then proceeded to do a cursory mop-up job of the bathroom.

"You missed a spot over there," Flynn indicated with his cane.

Charlie resisted the urge to dump the bucket over the elder's head. "It should be dry in an hour or so," he said, placing the mop and bucket in the corner.

"That's real nice of you, young fella," Flynn said. "I suppose you want me to pay you somethin'?"

"How about a beer?"

"Don't got no beer. Doctor won't let me drink it no more."

"A cup of coffee?"

"Got that," Flynn said. "What else?"

"A little information."

Flynn took a few seconds to ponder that. "Let me take my leak, an' we'll talk about it."

Once his emergency was put to rest, the old man took Charlie into the kitchen and made him a cup of instant coffee. He even gave him some Fig Newtons. "What kind of information you lookin' for?" he asked, as they sat across from each other at the kitchen table.

Charlie pushed some of the breakfast dishes out of his way to make way for his coffee cup. "I'm trying to find somebody," he said, "and I think you might be able to help me."

"As long as it don't cost me nothin'."

"Ever know somebody named Harlow? Robert or Bobby Harlow?"

Flynn answered immediately. "Nope."

"You sure? It was probably a long time ago. 1978, to be exact."

"I may be an old fart, kiddo, but I got a good memory for names and faces. I've lived in this house for near forty years, and no Harlow ever lived around here."

"How about where you worked?"

"He weren't in the oil fields." He took a bite out of his Fig Newton. "I'm not supposed to eat these. The seeds get stuck in my dentures," he said, sipping his coffee. "What do you want him for?"

"He's inherited some money."

"Lucky bastard." Flynn suddenly turned sullen. "You know, when I had my accident, I could've made me a bundle off the company. There were no question that their rig was no good. But, this 'friend' up in the front office sent me to some cheap, no-good lawyer. Hell, them big corporate fellas ran right over him."

"That's too bad," Charlie said. He was beginning to get impatient with the old man.

"Wound up with a lousy fifteen thousand after the doctor bills."

"Mr. Flynn," Charlie said, taking charge of the conversation. "Back in 1978, did you own a 1976 Ford station wagon?"

"*Ha!*" Flynn shouted, startling Charlie. "Did you finally find it?"

"What?"

"It was stole. Ethel, my wife, left the keys in it one night, and the next morning it was gone."

Charlie crossed his fingers. "When was this?" he asked.

"It was in 1978," Flynn said, thinking out loud. "The spring. May, maybe."

Charlie bounced down the steps of Flynn's porch and headed for the Thunderbird. "I'm *not* crazy," he thought, his mind overflowing with ideas. "I got the car. I saw a '76 Ford station wagon with a certain license plate, and *that's* what it turned out to be. I may not be able to prove that Harlow stole it, but *I got the car*."

Everything made sense. Harlow was a clever man. He was too smart to take his own car to kill Moreno. After all, what if he'd been seen? He could've taken Flynn's station wagon, done the deed, then dumped it in a river, or out in the desert someplace.

Charlie pulled away from the curb, and then made a U-turn in the middle of the block. He checked his watch. It was nearly four. If he hurried, he could see Jenny before he left for the airport.

———

123

Just as the Thunderbird rounded the corner, a steel gray Mercedes pulled out from a parking space across the street from Flynn's house. It had been situated there ever since Charlie had gone inside.

"Make sure you don't lose him," the man in the back seat said to the driver.

CHAPTER TWELVE

Charlie flushed the toilet, just as he heard the front door open.

"Hello! I'm home," he heard Jenny call out.

"Right in the nick of time," he thought, glad that she wouldn't discover that he hadn't walked Roger. He watched the evidence swirl down and disappear into the bottom of the bowl.

"I bought the two juiciest steaks." She entered the bedroom carrying a bag full of groceries. "What's this?" she said, noticing his open suitcase on the bed.

Charlie emerged from the bathroom, toilet articles in hand. He glanced in her direction and wished that she hadn't worn that tight yellow sweater, or that wisp of hair didn't cling to her forehead like it did. "I'm catching the seven o'clock plane back to L.A." He avoided eye contact. "Business."

"So glad you could drop by," she snapped, not bothering to hide her disappointment.

She turned her head away. Charlie knew that she was trying to avoid crying in front of him. He wrapped his arms around her and thought that maybe it would've been easier if he'd made his getaway earlier and left just a note behind.

"I'll be back," he said. "I'm in Dallas all the time."

He couldn't believe he was saying this to her.

"This isn't a motel, Charlie."

He turned her around to face him, and saw that the floodgates had let loose. "I know," he said, wiping her tears with his handkerchief. He took the bag of groceries from her and placed it on the bed. "I thought last night was one friend helping another."

"*I* thought we were working on a relationship." She spoke with a coolness that he hadn't noted in her before.

"That's gotta be the most overused word in the English language," he said, his automatic defense system going into operation. "'Relationship'." He took the cue to turn away from her and move to the bed to finish packing. "Whatever happened to *affair*? That was much more romantic."

Usually, he got a charge out of obscuring an issue and putting his accuser on the defensive. He didn't like himself for what he was doing to Jenny. Caring about a woman was new for him.

He shut his suitcase and headed for the living room. As he opened the front door, he turned back to look at her. She was standing in the bedroom doorway, trying to smile. "See you," she said.

"*Shmuck!*" he heard his gut shout. "Don't let this one get away."

"Shit!" He dropped the suitcase and hurried back to her. "I'm sorry," he said, after they'd embraced for a full minute. "I didn't want to hurt you." They kissed for another minute, and then embraced again.

"What's wrong, Charlie?"

"Jenny," he said, sitting her down on the sofa, "I really like you. Maybe we *could* have a...relationship."

Seeing more tears form in her eyes, he hesitated.

"Fuck that!" he continued, throwing caution to the wind. "I'm crazy about you. I want to be with you. But, not now."

"Why?"

"I'm into something. I can't let go of it."

"What is it?"

"Top secret for now," he shrugged. "It could be dangerous. No 'innocents' allowed." He kissed her again, then stood up and headed back to his suitcase. "Let me wrap it up, then I'll come back here and we'll spend some time together."

"Does this have anything to do with your out-of-body experience?"

"That's where it started." He checked his watch. "I'll call you," he said. Before she could reply, he was out the door.

Charlie dropped the Thunderbird at Hertz, and then stepped out onto the sidewalk to catch the tram to the airport terminal. He'd been berating himself about Jenny ever since he'd left her apartment. Humming the *Raiders March*, he decided that guilt was non-productive. He began to think about his next move in his Harlow investigation.

He knew he'd come to a virtual dead end in Dallas. He'd developed some interesting background information and some fascinating circumstantial possibilities, but the fact was that he'd been unable to uncover one piece of tangible evidence against the political candidate.

He had one last idea...a daring long shot. If it worked, things might turn out all right after all.

The tram stopped at the curb and its doors opened. "Delta?" Charlie asked.

The Chicano driver nodded. "Yes sir," he said, rubbing at the two-day stubble on his acne-scarred face.

Charlie climbed aboard the empty bus, stowed his bag in the luggage rack and selected a seat toward the rear. He picked up a discarded copy of *National Enquirer* on the seat next to him. A story about Lindsay Lohan caught his interest.

He didn't notice that the driver was watching him through his rearview mirror.

He also didn't notice that the driver passed by the waiting passengers at the next tram stop.

He was still unaware when the bus turned off the airport concourse and headed back toward the city.

He finished the Lindsay Lohan story and glanced out the window. He didn't recall there being any industrial buildings on the concourse. "*Hey!*" he shouted to the driver, realizing that the tram had left the airport.

The driver scratched at his stubble.

Charlie got out of his seat and walked up to the driver. "What the hell is this?" he demanded. "I got a plane to catch."

The driver reached inside his jacket and produced a handgun.

Charlie blanched. He didn't know the weapon's make or caliber, but it looked damn big.

The driver smiled. "We're going for a ride," he said.

Charlie tried to regain his composure. "Don't I, at least, get a black limousine?" he quipped, as he sat in the seat opposite the driver.

The driver smiled again, but didn't respond. Charlie wondered if Crock Mason had sent him.

———

128

They proceeded in silence for the next couple of blocks, until the driver pulled the tram over to the side of the road and stopped next to a steel gray Mercedes. He opened the front door. Charlie rose to his feet. "Stay seated, please," the driver said, leveling his weapon at him.

Charlie caught sight of the two men who got out of the car. They looked like prosperous businessmen, attired in expensive western-styled suits. Except that they had on dark sunglasses...the kind that prevented you from seeing the wearer's eyes.

Charlie knew that Crock Mason hadn't sent them. More likely, they'd been sent by some character from *The Sopranos*. He knew that he was in deep trouble.

The men climbed aboard the tram and the driver maneuvered the vehicle back out into the traffic. The apparent leader of the pair was of slender build and in his early fifties. Charlie thought he was kind of handsome, in a swarthy sort of way.

"Mr. Parsons?" The man extended his hand and a friendly smile that revealed a crooked front tooth. "Or, is it Powers?"

"You got it right," Charlie shrugged, getting to his feet. He wished that he could see the man's eyes. "What's going on here?"

"Please join me at the back of the bus."

"First," Charlie began to insist, "I want to know what's going...." He looked up at the other man and stopped mid-sentence. He was a few years older than his boss. And he *wasn't* smiling. His expression was saying, "Do what you were told, asshole."

Charlie surveyed the bulky frame, accented by a well-flattened nose. Without doubt, the man made Pete

Harlow look like a dwarf. Indeed, Charlie figured that he now had a pretty good idea what King Kong would look like in a suit.

"All will be explained at the back of the bus," the leader said.

Charlie found the seat where he'd left the *National Enquirer*. The leader sat opposite him, and his "muscle" planted himself two or three seats away. "Mr. Powers," the leader said, "why are you investigating my father's murder?"

Charlie didn't attempt to hide his surprise.

"I'm Freddy Moreno," the man explained.

"I'm...I'm writing a book." Charlie tried to appear calm.

"You're writing a book like I'm President of the United States." Moreno's snigger was like ice. "You make your living by ripping-off the movie studios."

"I've got literary ambitions."

Moreno's sigh reminded Charlie of the way his mother used to sigh when she was losing patience with him. "Mr. Powers," he said, "I don't want to waste my time and you don't want to miss your plane. So, let's do this like a quiz show."

Out of the corner of his eye, Charlie could see the "muscle" start to smile. He didn't like the smile.

"If you give me the right answers," Moreno continued, "you may get a prize. *But*, if you miss, Eddie will break your fucking fingers off."

Eddie's smile had turned into a broad grin.

"Wanna play?"

"I'm good at geography," Charlie said. He discovered that he'd forgotten how to chuckle.

Again, Moreno delivered his icy little laugh. "That's the spirit," he said, chewing at his inner lower lip. "But, the category is history. Why are you investigating my father's murder?"

Charlie figured he'd better try for the prize. "If I tell you, you won't believe me," he said.

"Try me. I'm very gullible."

"I...I had an out-of-body experience."

Moreno glanced over at Eddie, and then turned back to Charlie. His voice was without emotion. "You had an out-of-body experience?"

"That's right. I *saw* the shooting"

Moreno contemplated him for a very long moment, then, quite calmly, he called, "Eddie!"

"*It happened!*" Charlie yelled, as the muscle got out of his seat and started toward him. He glanced out of the moving tram. They were still driving around in an industrial area. There was nobody out there he could call to for help. "I swear to God!"

Moreno suddenly seemed interested. He signaled Eddie to stay put.

Charlie pressed the moment. "Check with the hospital," he said. "Ask the doctor. Goldstein was his name."

Moreno chewed on his lip again. "Tell me about the... 'shooting'."

"You believe me?"

"No," Moreno said. "But, I think *you* believe you."

As he'd done with Brenda and Professor Boyd, Charlie related the story of the chase, and the auto accident, and his subsequent journey into the astral plane of existence. Throughout the saga, Eddie listened with an amused curiosity and Moreno continued to make a light meal out of his inner lower lip.

"He picked up the suitcase and ran off," Charlie concluded. "It was full of money, wasn't it?"

Moreno ignored the question. "You didn't see the killer's face?"

"The man was in the shadows," Charlie lied, figuring he was out of immediate danger. He'd decided to keep a couple of his cards face down. "He *may* have had a beard."

"Harry Rocklin?" Moreno suggested to Eddie. The muscle shrugged and shook his head.

"Mr. Powers," Moreno said, "you still haven't told me *why* you're pursuing this investigation. Aside from your thirst for knowledge, what's in it for you?"

"You checked me out," Charlie answered. I'm after a quick buck." Moreno's noncommittal expression prompted him to continue. "If I could prove my story, there could be a book in it, couldn't there? Maybe even a bestseller."

Charlie began to like that idea. "Maybe I *could* write a book," he thought.

"My father and I were very close," Moreno mused. "He even took me fishing once."

Charlie wasn't sure how he should react to that last comment.

Moreno handed him a card with only a phone number printed on it. "If you should discover *any* information that might help me find his murderer...."

"You got it," Charlie interrupted.

"I'll make it worth your while." Moreno got up and, followed by Eddie, headed toward the front of the bus. "Harry Rocklin was in Chicago that week," he said to the muscle.

The tram had returned to the spot where the Mercedes was parked. "See that Mr. Powers makes his plane," Moreno told the driver.

The two men stepped off the tram, then, a moment later, Moreno stepped back on. "What's your *real* name?" he called to Powers.

"Charlie Powers."

"*What is it*?" he persisted. "Polanski? Polischeck? I know a Jew boy when I see one."

"Pollack," Charlie admitted.

"Why'd you change it?"

"Powers looks better on a marquee."

Moreno shook his head. "Don't be ashamed of your heritage, Mr. Pollack."

As the tram headed back toward the airport, Charlie watched through the rear window, as the two men got into the Mercedes. He was intrigued with Moreno's proposition and its financial possibilities.

He just wondered what the guy was *really* after.

CHAPTER THIRTEEN

"This is insane," Brenda said, as Charlie maneuvered his Mercedes into the parking spot. "How can you make such a fool of yourself?"

"Humor me."

"It's a public meeting."

"They won't know who asked the question."

He turned off the motor and looked across the street at the American Legion meeting hall. Already several dozen people had entered the wood frame building, a former World War II armory. A like number were standing on the sidewalk outside. The paper banner over the door read: "Meet ROBERT HARLOW Tonight."

The first thing Charlie had done when he'd returned from Dallas two days earlier was to call Harlow's local campaign office. "When's his next local appearance?" he'd asked the girl who'd answered the phone.

"That would be Friday, sir," she'd answered. "In Woodland Hills."

Charlie remembered that Woodland Hills was somewhere out in the west end of the San Fernando Valley.

"How much more time are you going to waste on this wild goose chase?" Brenda had asked when he'd first told her of his plan.

"Moreno didn't think I was crazy," he'd replied. "What's *he* got to lose?"

"Babe," he'd agreed, "you're right...absolutely right. Even with the license number checking out, I got nada. Zilch. Nothing concrete I can use against this guy."

"Then why go to that meeting? Let's go to a movie instead."

He'd sat her down in an armchair, and then knelt so that he could look her right in the eye. "I want his reaction," he'd said. "I want you to see his reaction. If it's a blank, then so be it. I'll quit. That's a promise."

She'd leaned back in the chair, resigned to the fact that there was no way she was going to talk him out of his scheme. "Mind if I sit on the other side of the room?" she'd asked.

Charlie locked the Mercedes and crossed Fallbrook, heading toward the meeting hall. Reaching the curb, he noticed that Brenda had lagged behind him. She was still standing by the car. He motioned for her to hurry along. She pointed to her watch, indicating that she'd be there in a minute.

"She really doesn't want to sit with me," Charlie muttered, as he walked to the entrance.

"Good evening." The older gentleman greeting people at the doorway was wearing a sharp blue blazer with some sort of nautical insignia embroidered on it, a cravat and a big "Vote for Harlow" button. Charlie figured he'd either been imported from an Orange County yacht club or was a retired actor from the nearby Motion Picture Country Home.

"Write down any questions you might have," the greeter said, indicating a card table with paper and pencils just inside the entrance. "Mr. Harlow will be happy to answer them."

"Thank you." Charlie decided that anyone with such a crisp resonant voice had to be a former bit player. He took a slip of paper from the card table; printed out the question he'd prepared and dropped it into a large fishbowl.

The interior of the hall had all the charm and warmth of an army barracks. The floor was concrete. The walls, except for a small trophy case and a couple of patriotic banners, were bare. At one end of the large room, facing about fifteen rows of metal folding chairs, was a low platform that accommodated four chairs, a small table and a podium with microphone attached.

Charlie found himself a seat near the center aisle that gave him an unobstructed view of the podium. He took a moment to peruse the mixture of faces in the nearly filled hall, and then chuckling softly, bet himself that he could pick out all the grass roots Harlow supporters.

They were ones who hadn't come dressed in casual garb. The men were in their three-piecers, and each of the ladies had a corsage pinned to her best suit or cocktail dress. This combination of gregarious Generation-Xers and laid back elders sat in the first four rows of the auditorium, ready to provide the soon-to-arrive candidate with one hell of a cheering section.

Charlie straightened his tie as his attention zeroed in on a frosted redhead in her mid-thirties. Wearing a bright pink suit and pink blouse, like she'd just come from a Mary Kay Cosmetics convention. She was up on the platform, apparently giving instructions to two of the men. Her manner made Charlie think of a Marine drill sergeant who had just graduated from charm school.

"She's got to be the head honcho," he mused, watching the extravaganza of pink move down to dictate some orders to the cheering section. "I'll bet she even orders her husband around in bed."

Brenda came in, finally. Charlie motioned to her to join him. She scowled and turned away, taking a seat in the row behind him.

He glared at her, slowly metamorphosing his features into the Basset hound pout that had never failed to pull a giggle from her.

Not amused, she again averted her gaze.

He continued to milk the expression. Then he saw that the gray-haired lady seated next to him was looking at him as if he were a cretin. Embarrassed, he smiled at her, crossed his legs and turned front.

Brenda giggled.

"Ladies and gentlemen," the pink lady was at the microphone, attempting to lower the level of jabbering that permeated the hall. "Can I have your attention, please?" Gradually the room began to quiet. "I think our guest of honor *has arrived*."

A dapper, smiling Robert Harlow appeared in the doorway, wearing a trim blue blazer, gray slacks and a red silk tie. Charlie thought that his face was slightly narrower than in the newspaper photographs, but this was definitely the man he'd seen blow away Vito Moreno.

Two companions followed Harlow. One was a bespectacled man in his fifties, who looked like a New England banker. Charlie decided he was Harlow's campaign advisor. The other was a big, much younger, fellow with an angelic face. Charlie pegged him as the bodyguard.

The candidate paused at the entrance and patted back a strand of his blondish hair. The audience rose to its feet to applaud him. "Give 'em hell, Bobby!" Charlie said quietly, as he stood up and clapped with a more modest enthusiasm. He saw that Brenda was also standing.

"Isn't he *wonderful*?" the gray-haired lady in the next seat said to him.

"He's extraordinarily amazing!" Charlie deadpanned. He wondered why she didn't pluck those hairs out of the mole on her chin.

The woman nodded with gusto, then turned back to watch the pink lady escort Harlow up to the platform. His two companions moved to the back of the room.

As the spectators continued to applaud, Charlie faced front to watch Harlow shake hands with the two local men on the platform. He didn't see the massive man with bruises and bandages on his face enter the auditorium.

Pete Harlow felt uncomfortable in a jacket and tie. He glanced around the room, and then lumbered over to an empty seat near the back wall.

The dignitaries took their seats on the platform, and the pink lady moved to the microphone. She stood there beaming with enthusiasm, until the crowd had quieted and resumed their seats.

"Ladies and gentlemen," she began, "I'm Charlene Faye. I want to welcome you to this gathering of the Valley Voters League." An electronic squeal emitted from the mike. "Oh, my!" she said, tapping the instrument with her pencil. The noise ceased, and she continued. "The purpose of our bi-partisan organization is to give you voters an objective view of the candidates and the issues. An informed voter is an intelligent voter."

"Wanna bet?" Charlie muttered under his breath.

"Tonight's guest is Robert Harlow, candidate for governor." She waited for another burst of applause to die out. "Mr. Harlow was born in Texas, and came to California in the early 1980s. He's a successful building contractor, and has served on various city and state committees dealing with housing. So, without further delay...I give you Mr. Harlow."

Harlow stood up and took the two or three steps to the podium. He beamed his perfect smile again. Charlie wondered if he'd had his teeth capped.

The audience, led by the cheering section in the front rows, got to their feet again and applauded. Charlie grumbled to himself, then followed suit.

The candidate offered his hand to Mrs. Faye, who clutched it for a lingering moment before returning to her seat. He faced the audience, still sporting that wide, friendly smile.

Charlie had to admit that even with those cold blue eyes, that good ol' boy from Texas was a handsome bastard and had one hell of a lot of charisma. He just wondered how that charm would fare after Harlow had heard his question.

"Thank you. Thank you very much," Harlow began after the current round of applause had finished. "I love the San Fernando Valley. The people here are all very warm...very friendly." More applause. "I've prepared no speech for tonight...."

Two people clapping and cheering from the back of the hall interrupted him. "*You* must be backing my opponent," he quipped, garnering some mild laughter from the crowd.

"I see a fishbowl full of questions by the door. They should give me enough opportunity to spout off. So, if you'll bring them forward, we'll begin."

The old greeter from the door carried the fishbowl up to the platform and placed it on the table next to Harlow.

"Mrs. Faye," Harlow said, turning to his hostess, "if you would please do the honors."

Charlie leaned forward in his seat, as Mrs. Faye reached into the fishbowl and picked the first slip of paper. Her facial expression conveyed her approval of the question. She read it like she was performing a public service announcement: "How would you curb the increasing incidents of gang violence in our communities?"

"That's a good question on a very disturbing subject," Harlow said, folding his arms. "What we have to remember is that gang violence is merely a symptom. What we have to address is the disease...."

Charlie covered his mouth and yawned, as he wondered how many times in the campaign the candidate had already given his prepared answer on this topic. He craned his neck to get a better view of the fishbowl. It looked to be three quarters full. Since he'd come in fairly late, he figured that his question might be close to the top. With luck, the pink lady should get to it soon, unless she started drawing queries from the bottom.

He glanced over at Brenda. She appeared to be interested in what the man was saying. "Maybe she'll vote for him," he mused.

The audience applauded, as Harlow completed his dissertation. "He's truly got the answer," the gray-haired lady in the next seat said to him.

"He truly does," Charlie nodded, figuring he'd make the old gal happy.

During the next twenty-five minutes, he kept looking toward the fishbowl while Harlow stated his views on capital punishment, state income taxes, reapportionment, the California state lottery and aid to public schools. "Come on, lady," he muttered, "get to my question."

"Let's stir this around a bit," Mrs. Faye said, reaching into the bowl for another slip of paper.

Harlow took a sip of water. "Good idea," he said.

"Shit!" Charlie began to wonder if his question might be missed altogether.

"'What was in...'?" Mrs. Faye stopped mid-sentence and squinted at the wording on the paper. "This looks like a joke," she said to Harlow.

Charlie snapped his full attention toward the podium. "Don't stop, lady," he murmured. "Read it!"

"We could all use a good laugh," Harlow said to the hostess. "Go ahead and read it."

The lady's expression asked, "Are you sure?"

"We're sure," Charlie said to himself.

"Just keep it clean," Harlow added, drawing a titter from the audience.

Charlie leaned forward in his seat and held his breath, as the woman looked again at the paper. "What was in Vito Moreno's suitcase?" she said. "Sounds like a question off of 'Jeopardy'." Her remark brought a few titters of uncertain laughter from the audience.

It was Harlow's eyes that betrayed him. For an ever so brief instant, they froze, apparently stunned by the question that had shaken ajar the doorway to his dark past.

"*I got him!*" Charlie whispered, wiping his moist palms on his pant legs. He glanced over at Brenda to see if she had caught Harlow's subtle reaction. Her expression was blank. Annoyed, he looked back at the candidate and fantasized that he would break down and confess.

Harlow started to smile. He shrugged his shoulders and replied, "His dirty underwear?"

The audience guffawed. Everybody enjoyed the moment, including Brenda.

"Isn't the answer on the back?" Harlow asked with mock disappointment. More laughter from the group.

Charlie didn't crack a smile. He watched Mrs. Faye reach her hand into the fishbowl for another question, and knew that he'd missed his chance. Harlow was slipping away from him.

He looked back at Brenda. The smug expression on her face was saying, "Satisfied, dummy?"

That really got him angry. She wasn't going to laugh at him, and neither was Harlow. He turned toward the front again, and did what he'd later remember as being the dumbest thing he'd ever done in his life.

"How about money?" he shouted.

Brenda cringed.

The gray-haired lady next to him reacted as if he'd just raped her mother.

In the rear of the room, Pete Harlow stopped picking his nose and looked to see who'd said that.

Charlie thought that Harlow appeared a bit shaken. The politician's smile had zapped off, then back onto his face.

Mrs. Faye turned her attention in Charlie's direction. "Questions are not allowed from the floor," she said.

Harlow, his composure recovered, turned and stared at him. His eyes squinted slightly, so that he could get a clear look at the interloper. Then, he smiled again, and Charlie felt like a dead man.

The audience's attention turned back to the platform. Brenda stood up and walked quickly toward the entrance.

All Charlie knew was that he had to get out of there...*fast*. He got up and moved down the row in pursuit of Brenda. "Excuse me," he said to the gray-haired woman, as he scooted by her. He kept his eyes focused on the exit, but he was aware of Harlow watching him every foot of the way.

Mrs. Faye read the next question. "Do you have a state program for earthquake safety?" she said.

"Being a builder," Harlow began like no incident had occurred, "I'm very aware of the hazards posed by the California earthquake menace...."

As he reached the door, Charlie glanced toward the back of the room. Harlow's bodyguard and campaign advisor were glowering at him, as was another man that he recognized.

Charlie blanched.

Pete Harlow made a gesture to his cousin on the platform, as if to say, "That's the one!"

"*Fuck!*" Charlie bolted out the door.

"You stupid ass!" Brenda said, as they hurried across Fallbrook toward the Mercedes.

"Did you see his reaction?"

"I saw it."

He pulled the keys from his pocket and unlocked the door. "*Now*, do you believe me?"

"I don't know what I believe," she said, climbing in on the passenger's side. "But, all of a sudden, I'm very frightened to know you."

Charlie didn't want to admit to her that he was sharing some of the same feelings. He started the engine, and looked to see if it was clear to pull out from their parking spot.

In the car's side mirror, he spotted Pete Harlow and the campaign advisor standing out in front of the meeting hall. The campaign advisor appeared to be copying down his license number.

CHAPTER FOURTEEN

He was ready to kill her.

Charlie scanned the contents of the crowded shelf, moved a bottle or two and lifted the tub of margarine to see if the tin foil-wrapped prize might be buried underneath.

There was no question about it. The pork chop was gone.

The sneaky bitch had stolen it while he was in the shower, or out walking Odif. And, she *knew* that he'd wanted it. He'd even told her when they'd cleaned up after dinner. *That's* what made the act so reprehensible.

He looked at the kitchen clock. It was ten after three. He was hungry...wide awake...and Brenda, the glutton, was in the bedroom sawing wood like a lumberjack.

He considered scrambling some eggs, but decided that scrubbing out the frying pan would be too much work. He settled instead for a slice of Swiss cheese, then readjusted the belt on his robe, and walked out into the living room. Odif was curled up by the fireplace, fast asleep. "Go ahead," Charlie said to the dog, "enjoy your rest. *I'm* going to be a zombie in the morning."

The guilt trip didn't work. The dog wagged his tail once, but did not open his eyes. Charlie plopped down onto the sofa.

The ride home from the meeting had left him on edge. He knew he'd screwed up there. He knew he hadn't played it smart. And Brenda hadn't let him forget it.

"You're caught between a rock and a hard place, aren't you?" she'd said with anger, as they'd headed east on the Ventura Freeway.

"How so?"

"Actually," she'd continued, "you got four choices. You can blackmail Harlow, and either get arrested or killed. You can call Moreno, and either get rich or get killed...."

"Stop already," he'd interrupted.

"You can call in the cops," she'd said, ignoring him. "They'd just lock you up for being crazy."

"That's not too bad," he'd responded with sarcasm. "What's number four?"

"Drop the whole thing and go back to being a respectable film pirate."

"Out of the question."

She'd turned away from him and submerged herself in her own thoughts.

"He did it!" he said. "The son-of-a-bitch did it."

"So what!" she snapped.

Charlie got up from the sofa and headed back to the kitchen. The cheese hadn't satisfied him. He knew there had to be *something* in the place that was good to eat.

"Consider the possibilities," he said aloud, recalling the conversation he'd had with Brenda just a few days earlier. He turned on the light and began rummaging through the pantry.

There was no question in Charlie's mind that Harlow was guilty. He'd seen the crime committed. What he'd witnessed matched up with the newspaper accounts of the case. The license number had checked. And Harlow's own reactions had shown him that the candidate had an extraordinary interest in the matter. All that was missing was actual evidence... physical proof that Robert Harlow had, indeed, killed Vito Moreno.

Short of a signed confession, Charlie now accepted that Brenda was right. No evidence existed. Harlow was too smart a cookie. He'd covered his trail very well.

Scratch the best seller. Forget about those appearances with Jay Leno. Writing another *All the President's Men* entailed gathering more hard facts than a journey through the "Twilight Zone" could provide.

So, how to turn a buck on all this?

Blackmail?

He could joke and fantasize about it, but Charlie knew that wasn't his bag. It was a dirty business. It was a dangerous business. And, after the panic...the fear he'd felt tonight at that meeting, he knew that he didn't have the stomach for it.

He wondered what Harlow was going to do with his license number. "Maybe I should get out of town for awhile," he considered.

He found a can of split pea soup, and decided to heat it up.

What about the police? The F.B.I.?

Forget it! Without evidence, it would be easier to write a book. He could always call that fiction, and claim that any resemblance to persons living or dead was purely coincidental.

That *was* an interesting idea. He wondered if he had the talent to write a novel. He wondered if he had the tenacity to finish a novel.

He decided to put that thought on a shelf and play with it for a while.

He shook some pepper into the soup, and stirred it around in the saucepan.

Then there was Fredo Moreno.

Why not call him? He had a right to know who killed his father. "If the law couldn't touch Harlow," Charlie rationalized, "then maybe justice could be served another way."

And besides, the hood had promised Charlie to make it "worth his while" if he passed any useful information on to him.

That's what he was going to do. He'd call Moreno and tell him what he knew. Moreno would lay a few grand on him. Twenty or twenty-five, maybe...*if* he played his cards right. He might even give him some protection.

Then he'd be out of it. He'd be safe from Harlow.

Charlie poured the soup into a mug and went back out into the living room. The desk clock read four a.m. That would make it only six in Dallas.

He wondered how late gangsters slept. In the movies, they always seemed to wake up in a rotten mood. The scene from *Public Enemy* of a pajama-clad Jimmy Cagney pushing a grapefruit into Mae Clarke's face kept popping in and out of his head.

He decided it might be wise to leave Moreno alone, at least 'til eight.

Taking a couple of swallows of the soup, he sat back down on the sofa and leaned his head back. Maybe he could grab a quick nap before he made that call. His mind was always at its sharpest right after he'd slept.

He put down the mug and shut his eyes.

He dreamed. He dreamed about Fredo Moreno. And he dreamed about Walter Huston.

The late character actor was costumed as a New England peddler from the middle 1800s. He wore a goatee and had that all too familiar wily twinkle in his eye.

He was that evilly seductive rogue, "Mr. Scratch," his Beelzebub role in *The Devil and Daniel Webster*.

They were chasing Charlie. Both Moreno and "Mr. Scratch".

But he wasn't Charlie Powers any longer. He was "Jabez Stone," the "Faust" of Stephen Vincent Benet's story.

He was running down corridors. Bland pastel green corridors with acoustical tile ceilings like those in a modern high-rise office building.

He'd turn a corner and they'd be there. He'd spin around and run the other way, and they'd be there, too. There was no escaping them or their mocking laughter. "We gotcha!" they'd cackle every time he'd run into them. "We gotcha!"

Then, "Mr. Scratch" opened up his coin purse. A moth flew out. Charlie recognized the creature from the movie. It was one of the devil's captured souls. Its frightened features were human. They were Charlie's features.

Moreno grabbed the pitiful thing as it tried to escape. He smashed it between his open palms.

"Shit!" Charlie awoke with a start, kicking the mug of soup off the coffee table. He tried to shake the sleep from his brain.

Noticing the muddy green goo sinking into the carpet, he went to the kitchen for a sponge. The dream crystallized again in his mind, as he cleaned up the mess. "I should stop seeing so many old movies," he thought. "Gotta change my frame of reference."

He took a bite from a fingernail.

The clock read a quarter-to-six. He chose not to wait any longer. He glanced at the card Moreno had given him and dialed the number. "What's he going to do if I wake him?" he asked himself, listening to the phone connection click into place. "Shoot me?"

He decided that this wasn't the time for black humor.

There were three rings before somebody picked up on the other end. "*Yeah?*" The voice sounded sleepy and annoyed. He recognized it as Moreno's.

Charlie had opened his mouth to speak, when a picture of the genial Mr. Scratch flashed across his mind again.

"Hello?" Moreno said.

Charlie hesitated. The dream's message had become clear to him.

"Who *the fuck* is this?"

Charlie couldn't really see himself as a moth. He hung up the receiver.

Odif sat up and looked at his master.

"What the hell do I do now?" Charlie said to the dog, as he started to reconsider his options. "About anything?"

Charlie was asleep in bed when he heard a phone ring somewhere in the distance. He buried his head under his pillow and prayed that Brenda would answer it.

"It's for you." The unusual shrill tone of her voice cut through his protective slumber and let in the harshness of the real world.

He rolled over and struggled to open his eyes. She was dressed in a snug blue blouse and jeans. "Who is it?" he asked, sitting up and forcing himself awake. His mouth tasted like he'd been eating the carpet.

"It sounds like Paul Di Mico."

The digital clock on the nightstand announced that it was 10:10. "Why's he calling so early?"

"Ask him," she said, handing over the phone. "I got an interview at Disney." She disappeared out the door.

Charlie stared at the instrument for a few moments before he picked up the receiver. "Hello?"

"Can you meet me tonight?" The traffic noises in the background indicated that Di Mico was calling from a phone booth.

"What do you got?"

"Tom Hanks' new one," Di Mico whispered.

"The usual spot?"

"Naw, parking lots are too public."

"Nobody pays any attention," Charlie objected. "They're safe."

"You want this picture or not?"

Charlie wanted the picture. "Where do we meet?" he asked.

"You know Longridge in the Valley?"

"Very well."

"Halfway up the canyon. Eight o'clock."

Charlie hung up the receiver, then stretched and arched his back. "Good deal!" he said aloud. He knew that a Tom Hanks flick could net him twenty or thirty big ones. Things were looking up.

He walked nude into the bathroom and turned on the shower. As he rubbed the shampoo into his hair, he wondered why Di Mico had gotten so brave all of a sudden.

CHAPTER FIFTEEN

Charlie turned onto Longridge and headed his Mercedes down the residential street toward the canyon. He slowed briefly when he passed the old Lou Costello house. Abbott and Costello had been his childhood idols, and he'd always had an urge to see inside the sprawling home where the fat comic had lived. Someday, when he had time, he figured he'd appear at the front door with some ruse that would get the present owners to give him a tour.

Termite inspector, maybe?

About halfway up the hill, he made a U-turn at the address he'd been given and pulled over to the side of the road in front of a plumber's mini-van. His watch read two minutes to eight. He turned off his lights, took a chew on his fingernail and began humming the *Raiders* march.

He'd only reached the second stanza when he spotted the pair of headlights proceeding up the hill. Recognizing Di Mico's Accord, he lowered his window. "Paul!" he called out.

The Honda pulled up next to the Mercedes. Di Mico swept the shoulder length brown hair out of his eyes and stuck his head through the window. "Hi!" he said, fidgeting with a pimple on his chin. "You got the money?"

"I got it," Charlie replied. He noted that his contact was a little paler and more glassy-eyed than the last time he'd seen him. "I thought things were too hot."

"I need the money."

Charlie knew why he needed the cash. At twenty-seven, the guy had the most expensive coke habit of anybody he knew.

Di Mico made a U-turn, and then parked behind Charlie's vehicle. "They're screening this print tomorrow afternoon," he said, as he opened his trunk.

Charlie examined the cans of 70mm film," then handed over the envelope. "I'll have it back here at midnight," he said. He thought it odd that Di Mico had simply stuck the envelope into his pocket. "You didn't count your money."

"I trust you."

The men transferred the film cans into Charlie's trunk, then without saying another word, Di Mico climbed into his Honda and took off down the hill. "He must be meeting his dealer," Charlie thought, slamming shut his trunk.

The drive over to Solley's Valley Video Service took fifteen minutes. The lights in the front of the corner one-storey building were off when Charlie arrived. He parked the Mercedes in the small lot in back, next to Solley's blue Cadillac Seville, and then knocked on the door.

"Who is it?"

Charlie felt like answering "F.B.I.," but since he had to have the print back to Di Mico by twelve, he decided not to give Solley's nervous stomach an excuse to act up. "Who do you think it is?" he said. "Santa Claus?"

Sixty-one-year-old Solley Schwartz still lived the life of a 1970s hippie. He sported a bushy beard, wore peasant shirts over his bulging belly, heavy gold chains around his neck and let the little hair he had left grow into a sparse version of an Afro.

Charlie liked Solley. He was a good friend. Somebody he could talk with, though he hadn't known him when he'd transformed himself over three years ago.

As the older man told it, he'd just come home from work one day, sat down at the dinner table and decided that he was tired of his wife's brisket. He emphasized his point by picking up his plate and smashing it against the wall. That, more or less, ended his marriage of over thirty years. He sold his thriving C.P.A. practice and moved in with a petite twenty-four year-old actress. They'd since wed and, just a few months ago, she'd presented him with a son. Solley was delighted with his new family, particularly since his grown children from his first union were having nothing to do with him.

"How many masters?" Solley asked, helping to carry the film cans into a large room containing two walls of every kind of video recording equipment imaginable, DVD, Digibeta, VHS and even an old Betamax.

"Give me four," Charlie said. "And burn me a DVD. I like Tom Hanks flicks."

As Charlie wandered around the room, sneaking peeks at labels on the various tapes lying about, Solley loaded a cassette into the Digibeta deck, and then put the first reel of the picture onto the TeleCine film chain. "Mind if I burn one for myself?"

"Go ahead," Charlie said. "But, I'm going to need the copies and the masters by tomorrow afternoon."

———

155

"Not a problem." Solley synchronized the film chain, and then turned it on. The film-pirating process had begun.

Charlie would be there for two hours, or for whatever the running time of the movie might be. After that, Solley would give him back the print, which he'd return to Di Mico, while the dubs, or duplicate masters, were being run off from the Digibeta original. Over the next week or two, Charlie would sell these dubs to underground film distributors like Howard Loy, who would manufacture hundreds of illegal DVDs from them, which they would sell all over the world.

"So, how you doin', kid?" Solley asked, sitting at his cluttered desk in the back of the room. He reached under his shirt and scratched his belly.

Charlie pulled up a straight back chair and leaned against the wall. "Lots of confusion these days," he confessed.

"Simplify!" Solley chuckled. "That's what I did. I don't have to worry about nobody else's taxes anymore. I don't have to listen to my J.A.P. wife kvetch anymore. All I do is do video transfers, then go home and make love to my beautiful young shiksa wife. What else could a man ask for?"

"Beats me," Charlie smiled.

"You got female problems?"

"Yeah. I got a new one in Dallas that I'm goofy about, and one here that's a pain in the ass, but...." Charlie found he couldn't dismiss Brenda with a few miscellaneous words.

"But, what?"

"She can be a tough lady," he admitted, "but...she's always been there for me."

Solley shrugged his shoulders. "You just got one thing to worry about, kid."

"Yeah?"

"Make sure the Dallas gal don't visit Los Angeles, and vice versa."

Charlie forced himself to laugh. "Solley," he said, getting up and heading for the coffee machine in the hallway, "it's too bad you never became a psychiatrist."

"I'd've made a great shrink," Solley agreed. "I'd just tell everybody to simplify."

"What's the matter with this thing?" Charlie slapped the side of the coffee machine.

"I don't know. The repairman's coming Friday."

Charlie headed for the door. "There's a Seven-Eleven around the corner," he said. "You want something?"

"Black coffee," Solley said, strolling over to check on the film chain. "And bring me back a jelly doughnut."

Charlie shot a critical glance at his friend's overflowing gut. "You really *need* that doughnut," he said.

"Fuck you!" Solley smiled.

Charlie poked around the convenience store for about ten minutes, glancing through the latest issues of *National Enquirer* and *The Star*. "Don't you have any jelly doughnuts?" he asked the clerk, as he perused the remnants of that morning's bakery delivery.

The clerk didn't bother looking up from the copy of *People* he was reading. "What you see is what we got," he said, scratching at the stud in his right earlobe.

Charlie bought a couple of glazed doughnuts and two large coffees. Sauntering back toward Solley's, he paused at the corner to gander at a cute rear end that was crossing Victory. Then, he turned right and headed down the block.

He was mentally debating the pros and cons of his relationships with Brenda and Jenny -- trying to devise a way to both have his cake and eat it, too -- when he caught sight of the Valley Video building.

"Oh, fuck!" he said.

Something was very wrong. All the inside lights were turned on. And parked outside were three unmarked, but very official- looking cars.

He ducked into the dark doorway of an upholstery business, keeping his eyes fixed on the front of the building across the street. Seconds later, four men emerged from Solley's. Two of them were carrying the 70mm film cans. Two others were flanking a handcuffed Solley Schwartz. Charlie wasn't sure, but it looked like Solley might have been weeping.

"Shit!...Shit!...*Shit!*" Charlie muttered, wishing that he hadn't parked his Mercedes in Solley's parking lot.

The men put the film cans in one car and Solley in another, and then drove off. A moment later, two other men came out of the building. They turned off the lights and shut the door.

Charlie recognized one of them. He dropped the coffee and doughnuts.

"Let's stick around for awhile," Hal Stuart said. "The punk may come back."

Charlie glanced back up toward Victory. The trees along the street kept the sidewalk pretty much in shadows. Perfect cover. He decided to take the only logical course of action.

He ran.

"*Hey!*" Charlie shouted, spotting Brenda's Corvette cruising down Victory. He was surprised that she'd made it so fast, since he'd phoned her less than twenty minutes ago. He dashed out from the alley next to the Seven-Eleven and pounded on the side of her vehicle. Startled, she looked at him, and then unlocked the door.

"Turn on the heat," he shivered, shutting the door.

"Where's your jacket?"

"Left it in my car," he said. "Jesus, it's cold tonight."

"What now?" Her manner reflected the outside temperature.

"Did you drive by Valley Video?"

"Your car's still in the lot," she nodded, "but somebody's watching it."

"Damn it!"

"Shall we wake up your favorite lawyer?"

"*Fuck! Shit!*" he exploded. "Who the hell could've tipped them?"

"Darling," she said with a smugness that further irritated him, "you *know* they've been after you."

"Drop dead!"

"You're welcome."

It took him a few moments to understand what she was getting at. "I'm sorry," he said. "I didn't mean that." He reached out and stroked her cheek.

"Your hand's cold." she said softly.

"Thanks for coming out and getting me."

Stopped at a red signal, she turned to him. "Hell, Charlie, isn't it time you stopped playing Russian roulette?"

"This had to be a set-up," he said. He chewed on a fingernail.

"Probably."

"Maybe they were on to Di Mico."

Brenda waited in the Corvette while Charlie called his Warner Brothers contact from a phone booth in a Chevron station. He let the phone ring six times. Not even Di Mico's answering machine picked up.

"Let's see if he keeps our twelve o'clock appointment," he said, getting back into the car.

Driving over to Longridge, they didn't speak. Charlie pondered his situation, as he continued with his oral manicure, and Brenda left him with his own thoughts. "Stop here," he said when they'd reached the foot of the canyon. "I'll walk the rest of the way."

"How far is it?"

"About two blocks...uphill." He looked at his watch. "It's five to twelve. If I'm not back in thirty minutes...."

"I'll start raising bail money."

Charlie decided not to respond to her wisecrack. He got out of the car and began trudging up the gorge.

He wished that he'd dressed warmer. It was freezing in the canyon. Much colder than in the flat part of the Valley. He rubbed at his bare arms and quickened his pace, as he passed by the junior estates lining the narrow road.

Keeping in the shadows, he rounded the bend. He saw the Honda Accord about fifty yards up ahead. It was parked under a tree behind a plumber's mini-van. He couldn't see if anybody was inside. Then its lights flashed on and off. That was the signal.

Charlie hurried across the road toward the car. Half of him was tempted to slug Di Mico for being careless, while the wiser half knew that they had to find a way to cut their losses.

Drawing nearer to the vehicle, he could make out a dark form sitting behind the wheel. "Paul," he said, "who the hell did you...."

The car door opened. The driver got out.

Charlie froze.

Hal Stuart grinned. "Hello, asshole," he said.

CHAPTER SIXTEEN

Miles Goodman signed the release form and passed it back to the desk sergeant. He couldn't help staring at the bent wart growing out of the side of the older man's nose. "Why doesn't he have it burned off?" he wondered.

The sergeant ran his fingers over his bald pate, as he looked over the document. "How'd you pull this off, counselor?" he asked, giving the imposing 6'1" attorney's scruffy muttonchops a wary once over.

"Pulled *what* off?"

"You got your boy out on an O.R., and he ain't even been in front of a judge yet."

"I got friends in high places," Goodman smiled. He zipped up his leather jacket and rubbed his hands together. "Don't you turn on the heat in this place?"

The sergeant glowered. "Feels warm to me," he said. We'll have *Mr.* Powers up here in a few minutes."

Goodman thanked him, then glanced over at the wooden bench in the reception area. He decided not to sit between the middle-aged Chicano couple, waiting for word on their gang member son, and the young black woman, hoping to bail out the drunken husband that had just given her a shiner. He'd divorced himself from that kind of misery two years ago when he'd phased out his criminal law practice in favor of contracts and litigation.

"Charlie, you shmuck," he thought, setting down his attaché case and leaning against the wall, "I'm thirty-five. I'm getting too old for this shit. Why couldn't you have gotten yourself arrested during regular business hours?"

In a daytime arrest, Powers would have been brought downtown almost immediately and presented before a U.S. Magistrate where bail would be set. Goodman much preferred the Federal atmosphere. There were no street gangs there. There were no pimps. There were no wife beaters. Just "nice" white-collar criminals, like tax evaders, copyright infringers and Mafia chieftains.

However, after hours, it was F.B.I. policy to leave their prisoners in the nearest holding facility until the next morning when the U.S. Marshal would transport them to the Federal court. In this instance, the nearest facility was the North Hollywood precinct of the Los Angeles Police Department.

The wall clock told Goodman it was five minutes to three in the morning. He had a date to play racquetball at ten. There was a hundred bucks and the "championship of the universe" riding on this rematch with the county commissioner. "*I'm* the shmuck," he muttered. "That's what I get for having a client as a friend."

He'd met Charlie at a cocktail party three years ago. It was one of those Beverly Hills media events to celebrate the birth of something that that community really needed: a new boutique. Goodman was there because he'd drawn up some contracts for the Swiss gay couple that owned the place. Charlie's excuse was that he'd been dating the lady who was catering the function.

Under a spiral staircase where they'd both taken refuge from the mass of third-rate celebrities, freeloaders

and paparazzi that filled the shop, they'd struck up a
conversation about the phony aspects of show business,
the law and life in general. They'd found that they had
much in common.

"You ought to get rid of those glasses," Charlie
suggested, indicating the attorney's thick black frames.
"You'll win more jury cases."

Goodman had started to laugh and almost choked
on a shrimp hors d'oeuvre he had in his mouth. "What are
you talking about?"

"They make you look like a corporate lawyer.
Nobody likes a corporate lawyer."

"What am I supposed to do? Bump into the
furniture? I'm half blind without them."

"Did you ever see Gregory Peck in *To Kill a
Mockingbird*?" Charlie asked.

"A long time ago. What about it?"

"You remember those cheap wire-frame spectacles
he wore?" Charlie had attempted a facial impersonation of
the somber actor. "They made him look so warm...so
folksy...in the courtroom scene. The jury was crazy about
him."

Goodman pondered a moment. "As I recall...," he
began. "Didn't Peck lose that case?"

"Sure," Charlie had replied without hesitation.
"They convicted his client, but they *loved* him."

Charlie had enchanted Goodman. The lawyer had
found his sense of humor and nonchalant attitude toward
life to be a rather refreshing diversion from his
conservative world of contracts, courtrooms and
litigations.

They played tennis and racquetball together. They went to football and baseball games together. They lunched together once or twice a month.

Goodman's wife, Laurie, thought his new wire frame glasses were rather "cute", but she didn't approve of her husband's new friend. Nor did she like it when Miles had grown his muttonchops. "Charlie says they'll 'add character'," he'd explained.

"He's a cheap little crook," she'd argued that time he'd gotten Charlie off on *The Incredibles* deal. "Your parents didn't send you through law school to become friends with people like him." Yet, come Christmas, she would happily accept the bootlegged copies of Disney's *Song of the South* and Peter Jackson's *King Kong* that the 'cheap little crook' would send over for the Goodman kids.

Miles had even taken Charlie's suggestion about the glasses. He'd bought an inexpensive wire-framed pair and began wearing them in the courtroom. That last year he practiced criminal law, he started to win more cases than he lost, although he was hesitant to give the credit to his new eye prop.

"If it works, it works," Charlie had told him. "Why argue with success?"

Despite any misgivings he might have about the man's character, Goodman had to admit that Charlie Powers had certainly become a mildly fascinating influence in his life.

"Charlie," he said, as his client stepped out of the precinct's holding area, "you look like shit."

"I must smell like it, too," Charlie frowned, scratching at his arm, then at his ruffled hair. He avoided touching his soiled shirt and pants. "Some drunk decided to take a piss in there and he sprayed the joint."

Goodman took a whiff and nodded. "You're right. You'd better burn your clothes." He pointed to the exit. "Brenda's waiting in the car."

"How'd you get me out so fast?"

"I've got an old fraternity brother in the U.S. Attorney's office. He owed me a favor."

"What about Solley?"

"He's not my client, but he'll be out in a few hours."

"Thanks, Miles. I appreciate it." They stepped outside and Charlie took in a deep breath of air. "At least I can breathe out here," he said.

"Car's down the street." They headed down the walkway toward the sidewalk. "You're out on your 'own recognizance'. That means...."

"I know what that means," Charlie interrupted. "No bail."

"And *my* ass if you fuck up."

"Don't worry, counselor. I'm not going to fuck up," Charlie said, his voice tinged with a snarl. "I'm just going to have a talk with Mr. Di Mico."

"Friend Powers," Goodman said. He stepped in front of his angry client. "It's the middle of the night. Go home, take a shower and go to bed."

"My buddy got me sent to jail, damn it!"

"Stay away from him," the attorney insisted. "You're in enough trouble already."

"You're a good lawyer," Charlie said, trying to move around him. "You'll fix it."

"Maybe not this time. They got you on 'Candid Camera'."

Charlie hesitated and took a bite off his fingernail. "Where was it?" he asked.

———

166

"Hidden in a plumber's van."

"I *saw* that damn van," Charlie muttered. "My gut must've been out to lunch."

"What are you talking about?"

"Never mind."

"You know," Goodman said, "the motion picture industry is putting more and more pressure on Congress and the Justice Department these days. There's even some evidence that Al Qaeda and other terrorist groups sell bootlegged DVDs to help finance their activities."

"That's bullshit."

"Maybe so, but copyright infringement is no longer a laughing matter. You may be staring at two or three years in the slammer."

Charlie forced a smile. "Prove entrapment," he said.

"I don't know if I can," Goodman said. "They're getting a lot of convictions in these cases."

Charlie stopped smiling.

"You okay?" Brenda asked, emerging from her Corvette. Her nose warned her not to come too close.

Charlie nodded to her, then turned back to Goodman. "What about my car?"

"They'll release it out of impound. You just pay the towing charges."

"Fine," Charlie muttered. He opened the door of the Corvette.

"Mind me, Charlie," Goodman said. "Stay away from Di Mico."

"Yeah."

"Call me about four tomorrow. I'll have a better idea of what we're dealing with."

"Thanks, Miles." Charlie slammed the car door, and then rolled down the window. "I mean it. You've been a good friend."

"I'm sure we'll be able to work something out downtown," Goodman said, not really sure he believed that himself.

"Give my best to Laurie."

"*If* she'll let me back into the house," the lawyer said. "She didn't like my going out tonight."

"What else is new?" Charlie looked over at Brenda, who had just slid in behind the wheel. "Home, my good woman," he said.

Watching the Corvette move off down the street, Miles Goodman couldn't help but feel a bit depressed.

Charlie felt dirty. He felt even filthier than after he'd gotten out of that mud hole down in Texas. He had Brenda stop at an all night drug store, so that he could pick up some disinfectant soap and shampoo with which to shower. Then, after he'd spent a half hour washing and rewashing his body, he took Goodman's facetious advice and tossed his clothes into the trash.

Brenda was already asleep when he finally came to bed around four-thirty. He was grateful for the time to be left with his own thoughts. As he drifted off to sleep, he thought of Scarlett O'Hara's motto, "Think about it tomorrow. For tomorrow is another day."

Tomorrow came at ten the next morning for Charlie. The phone's shrill ringing nudged him awake. He reached out and grabbed the receiver off the hook, then buried it under the pillow.

"Hello?" He heard the muffled male voice through the goose down. "Mr. Powers?"

Forcing himself into a sitting position, he stared at the beige cord that stretched from the phone cradle to under the pillow and momentarily wondered how it got there.

"Hello?" The muffled voice was becoming more insistent.

"You'd better not be trying to sell me anything," he said to the caller.

"Is this Mr. Powers?" The voice was tinted with a touch of Texas.

"Yeah."

"Did you enjoy your evening?"

Charlie started to respond with "*What* evening?" then pictures of the previous night began to flash through his head like a slide show. "Who *is* this?" he said.

"*We* arranged the entertainment."

Charlie felt as if he'd been plunged into a vat of ice water. He opened his mouth to answer, but the words wouldn't come.

"Mr. Powers?"

Charlie managed to emit an "I'm listening."

"We *know* about your trip to Texas," the man said with a gentle sting. "Stay out of politics. It can be a dangerous business."

"Fuck off!" Charlie snapped, feeling a surge of false bravado. He slammed down the receiver and headed for the bathroom. After using the toilet, he splashed some water onto his face to wash away the remnants of sleep. He was drying off with a towel when he spotted his reflection in the mirror.

"I'm in deep shit," he said to himself.

CHAPTER SEVENTEEN

"I'm from Technicolor," Charlie said, pointing to the two 3/4 inch tape cassettes on the seat next to him. "I got a rush delivery for editorial."

"You know where to go?" the guard asked.

"Sure do."

The guard waved him through the gate "Park in any empty space."

Charlie drove his Mercedes onto the Warner Brothers lot, past the sound stages where Errol Flynn had once matched swords with Basil Rathbone, and where Bogart and Bergman had once made love in a nightclub called "Rick's". He drove by the commissary and along the old New York street set where the likes of Jimmy Cagney and Edward G. Robinson had once been mowed down by machine gun fire.

These were the stars of his youth, Charlie mused. The stars that his father had introduced him to via their VHS player. These were the real stars, real tough guys and strong women. Not like the wusses on screens today.

He found a parking spot next to one of the old wood frame editing bungalows. On another day, he might've locked his car and strolled along those backlot sets, then taken a peek inside one of the empty stages. Certainly he'd done that before on days that he'd been at the studio to interview for a role.

There were ghosts on those stages. Marvelous ghosts that he would've liked to have known. Now he only dreamed about them.

Charlie tossed his sport jacket into the car, then grabbed the tape cassettes and entered the editing bungalow. He looked about for a building directory. There was none.

"Can I help you?"

He glanced over at the blonde with the purple streak in her hair who was running an Avid in the editing room behind him. "Paul Di Mico?"

"Upstairs," she said, not taking her eyes off the small screen. "End of the hall."

Charlie glided up the steps. He could hear a film soundtrack on an Avid, as he moved down the short hallway toward the only door that was open.

Dressed in a black jeans and a light sweater with his long brown hair tied in a ponytail, Di Mico was pounding away at his Avid's keyboard, his slender back turned toward the door. "From the rear, the shithead almost looks like a woman," Charlie thought, noting the editor's lithe movements as he rearranged the sequence of shots on the movie he was editing.

Charlie slipped into the small room cluttered with 3/4-inch cassettes and shut the door. The soundtrack from the movie running through the Avid kept Di Mico unaware of his presence. He set the cassettes down on a chair and waited. "Do I pull his chair out from under him?" Charlie debated, "or should I be more diplomatic and kick him in the balls?"

Di Mico himself rendered Charlie's deliberations moot. Reaching for another cassette on his desk, he caught sight of his uninvited guest standing by the door. "*Jesus!*" he shrieked, jumping up from his chair. His foot entangled on the desk's caster. He tumbled backwards onto the floor, knocking over a pile of cassettes as he fell.

Charlie couldn't help but laugh. "I wish I had a picture of that," he said.

"You startled me." Di Mico tried to mask his embarrassment. He pushed the cassettes off his body and scrambled to his feet. "What are you doing here?"

"Guess," Charlie said. His smile had disappeared.

"I'm sorry." Di Mico averted his gaze. He bent over and started to restack the cassettes. "They *made* me do it."

Charlie let himself explode. He planted the heel of his foot on the editor's rear end. "*Fuck you!*" he said, watching Di Mico go sprawling into the cassettes again.

"Leave me alone, Charlie!" Tears were forming in Di Mico's eyes. He grabbed hold of the workbench and pulled himself to his feet.

"Who *made* you do it?"

Di Mico's hand found a letter opener on the desk. He pointed it toward Charlie in a feeble attempt to defend himself.

"What are you going to do with that?" Once more, Charlie allowed himself to smile.

"Get out of here!" Di Mico said, making small jabbing thrusts with the letter opener, as he backed into the corner.

"I will." Charlie started to move toward him. "In a minute."

"Stay away from me!"

"Who came to see you, Paul?"

Di Mico made a quick thrust with the letter opener. Charlie stepped to the side, grabbed his attacker's hand and smashed it into the Avid. "*Shit!*" the editor screamed, as he dropped his weapon.

Charlie brought his right fist down on Di Mico's nose. He heard bone crack. Blood spurted from both nostrils. Di Mico started to collapse. Charlie grabbed him before he hit the floor. He pushed him over the desk and held him there with an arm lock.

"Paul," Charlie said, recalling his experience with Moreno in Dallas, "let's do this like a quiz show. If you give me the right answers, you *might* get a prize." He increased the pressure on Di Mico's arm. "The prize is that I *might* not break your fucking arm off."

Miles Goodman set down the contract he was revising and answered his intercom. "Charlie Powers is on the line," his secretary said. "He's calling from a phone booth."

"Tell him I said to call at four" the attorney replied, not wanting to break his train of thought. "Tell him I don't know anything yet."

"He says it's urgent."

"Everything's urgent with Charlie." He picked up the phone. "What do you want, big shot?" he said, tossing his pencil onto the desk.

"I gotta see you, Miles," Charlie said.

"What's the matter?"

"I just saw Di Mico...."

"You *what*?!?" Goodman snapped. "Didn't I tell you to stay away from him?"

"That's not important, now."

Goodman felt his temper rising fast. "If I'm your attorney, Charlie," he said, "then you fucking well better do what I tell you to do."

"Listen to me," Charlie said.

"I'll listen to you, asshole, when you start listening to me." The lawyer slammed down the phone and leaned back in his chair. "Stupid, *stupid* jerk," he muttered.

He began to peruse the contract again, then tossed it aside. "Claudia," he said to his secretary through the intercom, "try to get Mr. Powers back, would you?"

"He was calling from a phone booth."

"Then leave a message on his answering machine." Goodman said, wondering how much damage the jerk had done to his case.

Hal Stuart checked his watch, as he stepped off the elevator into the underground parking area. He had an appointment over at the Motion Picture Association and he was running late. Searching his coat pocket for the keys, he trotted over to his Ford sedan.

"Hey, Stu!"

The agent turned and saw Charlie Powers hurrying across the garage toward him. "How'd *you* get in here?" he asked.

"I'm very resourceful," Charlie quipped, his usual zest noticeably absent.

"Humph," Stuart muttered. "We saw how resourceful you were last night." He found the keys and started to unlock his car. "It's amazing you got out so fast."

"My lawyer's pretty resourceful, too."

"What do you want, Powers? I'm in a hurry."

"I want to talk to you."

"Better talk to your lawyer first."

"He's pissed at me."

Stuart couldn't resist a guffaw. "I wouldn't want to compromise our case," he said, opening the car door.

"My arrest was a set-up, you know," Charlie said.

"Was it?"

"Two goons -- not F.B.I., not studio brass -- paid Di Mico a visit before he called you guys."

"Really?" Stuart was unimpressed.

"They threatened him. If he didn't rat on me, he'd lose his job...and his ass."

"Maybe those guys should get a medal." Stuart thought it was a pleasure to see Powers so dismayed for a change.

"Damn it!" Charlie snapped. "Listen to me! I'm liable to make you a big hero."

Stuart withstood the urge to lay his fist deep into Power's gut. "I don't want to hear your bullshit, Charlie," he said. "You've been laughing at us. You've been laughing at the whole fucking establishment for years. But, now we've nailed you, and *that's that*." He turned to get into his car. "Why aren't you laughing now, Charlie?"

"I know who killed Vito Moreno," Charlie blurted.

"Oh," Stuart chuckled, "we're back to that again."

"I *know*."

The agent could see that he was serious. "Okay," he said, "I'll bite. Who killed him?"

Charlie hesitated, and then answered, "Robert Harlow."

"*Harlow!?!*" Stuart said, reacting with a combination of shock and amusement. "The candidate for governor?"

"I know it sounds screwy, but just let me explain."

"Damn you!" Stuart grabbed Charlie by the front of his jacket and slammed him up against the car. "Isn't there anything in this world that you take seriously any more?" He again resisted the temptation to hit this punk.

Disgusted, he pushed him away and climbed into his car. "If you're going to start accusing people of murder," he said, closing the door, "think big. Why accuse Harlow? Why not the President? Why not the Pope?"

Charlie had never dealt well with frustration. "*I saw it happen*," he shouted.

Stuart started his engine. "When?" he asked with a chuckle. "Before or after your father met your mother?" He put the car into gear and stepped on the gas. "I got more important things to do right now."

"*Listen to me!*" Charlie screamed, as he watched the sedan head up the exit ramp and turn onto Wilshire Boulevard.

Charlie kicked the concrete support column. "*Fuck! Shit! Fuck!*" he mumbled, limping toward the exit.

Halfway up the ramp, he thought he heard something behind him. The sound of shoe leather on concrete. He stopped and looked back down into the garage. There didn't appear to be anyone there.

He began humming the *Raider's* march, as he hurried out onto Wilshire Boulevard.

"Do you have cartridges for this?" Charlie asked. He took the clip out of the Beretta and examined it.

The pawnbroker was a small, thin man in his late fifties, who wore a gray sweater and spoke with a Polish accent. There was a warm quality about him that reminded Charlie of his father. "Everything you need," he smiled.

"Okay, I'll take it." Charlie pulled a wad of currency out of his pocket. "Wrap it up." He peeled off the two hundred dollars that the man had asked for.

"First," the pawnbroker said, as he picked up the money, "you have to fill out the paper." He produced a pen and a pad of official-looking forms from under the counter. "*Then*, you can pick it all up on the 25th."

Charlie gripped the Beretta. "I need this today," he said.

"I'm sorry," the man said with some apprehension. "The law says I can't give you the gun for two weeks." He reached for the weapon. Charlie saw that his hand was trembling.

"What does *this* say?" Charlie asked. He threw an extra fifty onto the counter.

The pawnbroker spoke kindly. "Mister, I been here a long time. I don't break the law." He retrieved the weapon from Charlie's grasp, then handed back the money. "If you're in trouble, why don't you go to the police?"

Charlie decided not to burden him with his troubles. "Thanks," he said, as he left the store.

The big man with the angelic face punched the connect button on his cell phone. "He just come out of another pawnshop," he said to the person who answered. "They didn't sell him no gun there neither."

"You think that F.B.I. man believed him?"

"Didn't sound like it," the big man said, "but how should I know how them Feds think?"

"Mr. Powers is starting to become more than just a pain in the ass."

"Yeah."

"Maybe something should be done about him."

CHAPTER EIGHTEEN

"I don't believe it!" Brenda squealed into the receiver. She jumped up from the sofa and, carrying the phone, began pacing back and forth in front of the coffee table. "I thought they cast somebody else."

"'Somebody else' got pregnant." Her agent's voice had that echo-like quality rife with speaker phones. "She's *having* the baby."

"Thank God for motherhood."

"They're sending you over a script tonight. You fly to New York on Saturday. Start shooting Monday. Five thousand per episode. Seven out of thirteen episodes guaranteed."

"Wait a minute!" Brenda stopped pacing. Her smile disappeared. "When I tested, they said it was for *all* episodes."

"Brenda, honey," the agent said, "don't create problems. They'll probably use you in every episode anyway."

"I know that," she said, reaching into her robe pocket for a pack of cigarettes, "but that wasn't the deal."

The agent got off his speaker phone and picked up the receiver. "Are you looking a gift horse in the mouth?" he whispered. "They tested two other girls, you know."

"But they *want* me."

The phone was silent for a moment, and then the agent grumbled, "You want me to blow the deal?"

"Of course not, Timmy," Brenda said. "You think I'm stupid?"

"You had me worried for a minute."

"Just *nudge* them a little. You think you can do that, Timmy?"

"I'll give it a shot."

"Give it your *best* shot." Brenda hung up knowing that, in all likelihood, Timmy wasn't even going to try to get her a better deal. He'd call her back in the morning and tell her that they'd stonewalled him with a "take it or leave it."

She decided that she needed new representation. A *big* agency. One that was more interested in building her career into a multi-million dollar proposition, rather than just earning a commission on a job here and there. She figured that, with the series, she'd now be able to attract such an agency.

"I'm going to be on 'Law and Order'," she yelled, as she skipped into the bedroom to get ready for her acting class.

She stopped in front of the full-length mirror on the bathroom door and dropped her robe. "I got damn good tits," she said, examining her nudity. "I bet I can even get the cover of *Playboy*." She turned on the shower and stepped under the spray. "All I need is a good press agent, and I'll give Nicole Kidman a run for her money."

Toweling off a few minutes later, she thought of Charlie.

This was the opportunity that she'd been waiting for. Even if she only did the seven shows, that thirty-five thousand would give her the financial means to break away from him. She could get her own place. She could start dating some of the big wheels in the industry.

Producers, directors or studio execs who would take a special interest in her and her career.

"Goodbye, Charlie," she said, slipping on her bra and panties.

"*Shit!*" She knew it wasn't going to be that easy. She loved the guy, even if he was a dumb shit. Most of the men she'd been involved with were. She sure had a talent for picking 'em.

Still, Charlie was in trouble. "I'll see him through this thing," she rationalized, "*then* I'll leave."

She'd just finished putting on her lipstick when she heard him come in and start playing with Odif. "Hey, Charlie!" she shouted, as she pranced out into the living room. "*I got it!*"

"Got what?" He was stretched out on the floor, rubbing the dog's tummy.

"'Law and Order'."

"Oh, that's great," he said, trying to smile.

Brenda couldn't remember ever seen him looking so forlorn. She subdued her impulse to snap at his lack of enthusiasm. "What's the matter?" she asked.

"I'm fucked," he said, getting to his feet and crossing to the bar. "I just spent the last few hours sitting in the Los Angeles Art Museum, staring at a huge yellow canvas called 'Yellow.' Great meditation therapy. Everybody should try it." He grabbed a couple of ice cubes from the bar frig and dropped them into a highball glass. "And, the great revelation that I had was that I'm totally fucked."

"Maybe you should talk to Miles?" she suggested, not quite sure what he was driving at. "His secretary left a message on the machine."

"Miles is a long story." He poured himself a large scotch. "You want one?"

"I've got acting class."

"You'd better skip that tonight."

"Why"

"Just skip it." He plopped down onto the sofa.

"What the hell is going on?" she demanded.

He told her about the mysterious phone call that morning, his visit to Di Mico at the studio and his subsequent brief conversation with Goodman. By the time he'd begun to relate the gist of his confrontation with Stuart, Brenda had made her own journey to the bar and poured herself a double. "You could try going to the press," she suggested.

"Would they believe me?"

"There's always *National Enquirer*," she shrugged.

"No jokes, please."

Brenda finished her drink and poured herself another. "Who's joking?" she grumbled. "If they know about you, they probably know about me, too. That's not funny." She took another gulp of scotch, then let go of her brake.

"*You goddamn son-of-a-bitch bastard!*" she yelled. She flung her drink across the room at him. The glass missed, bouncing off the sofa. "Didn't you hear me?" she continued, throwing herself at him, fists flailing. "I just got cast on 'Law and Order.' *I just got cast on 'Law and Order'.*"

Charlie accepted her first two slaps, and then he caught her wrists and pulled her close. He wrapped his arms around her, as her body went limp. Her anger dissolved into sobs. "I'm sorry," he said. "I'm really sorry."

A few minutes passed before Brenda composed herself. She drew back from him, wiping her eyes and blowing her nose. Sitting on the floor cross-legged, she lit a cigarette. "What are we going to do, Charlie?" she asked finally.

"I'm not sure."

"Maybe you should call Moreno's son? Didn't he offer you 'protection'?"

"I thought about that," she said. "Decided not to."

"Don't tell me you're developing some 'character'." Her sarcastic tone seemed to be mixed with a tinge of respect.

He forced a laugh. "Screw 'character'! Those people can shoot me, too."

Brenda didn't smile. Instead, she got to her feet and headed back for the bar. "Hell, I don't want another drink," she said, changing direction for the kitchen. "I want a cup of coffee."

"We'll skip." He got up and followed her. "Disappear. I'll go to the bank tomorrow, and...."

"You're out on bail. Remember?" She poured a carafe of water into the Mr. Coffee and turned it on. "The F.B.I. will track you down in two minutes." Still bristling, she turned to look at him. "Besides, if you didn't hear me out there, *I* just got cast on 'Law and Order,' and I ain't gonna blow that."

His retort was waylaid by the ringing of the phone. Brenda grabbed the wall receiver. "Hello?" she said in the sweetest voice she could muster. There was silence on the other end. "Hello?" Brenda repeated. "Is anybody there?"

The caller's voice was hesitant...and female. "Is this the Charlie Powers' residence?"

"Who's calling, please?" Brenda asked, her eyebrow raised.

"Jenny Bradshaw."

Brenda handed over the receiver. "Do you know a Jenny Bradshaw?" She smiled, and Charlie knew he was in the shithouse.

"Hi, Jenny," he said, avoiding Brenda's cool stare. "How are you?"

"Okay. How are you?"

"Couldn't be better. What's up?"

"I just called to say...." She paused for a moment, then spit it out. "Charlie, who was that woman?"

"That was Brenda," he said, trying to sound casual. He could feel Brenda both laughing to herself and seething at the same time.

"Who's Brenda?" both ladies said simultaneously.

"A friend." He figured it was time to change the subject. "How's the weather in Dallas?" he asked.

"Do you live with her?" Jenny persisted.

Charlie didn't want to lie to her. "Jen," he said, "can I call you back? I'm a little busy just now."

"Please don't." He could tell she was trying not to cry. "I was just going to sleep." She slammed down the receiver.

Charlie stared briefly at the dead phone in his hand before he replaced it on the hook. "That was Jen," he said, without looking directly at Brenda.

Silence. Brenda stood leaning against the counter, arms folded.

"I met her in Dallas," he continued, groping for an acceptable explanation. "She's the one who hit me."

Brenda's tone was straight from the freezer. "And, what *else*?" she said, feeling like the world's biggest chump.

"Nothing! I swear." Charlie tried not to sound too desperate.

"Bullshit!" She wiped her hands on the dishtowel and headed for the living room. In a way, she rationalized, it was good that this had happened. It gave her the perfect excuse to bail out of this mess.

"Come on, Brenda," he said, standing in the kitchen doorway. "Don't go jealous on me now. I got problems enough."

Brenda grabbed her denim jacket from the coat tree by the front door. "I'm sure you can solve them," she said. "All by yourself."

"Can't we talk about this?"

"I'm going to acting class."

"Brenda, please don't go. I need you."

She knew she'd have to get out of there quickly, or she'd start sobbing again. "I'll talk to you later," she said, refusing to face him.

She opened the door, and then stopped. There was a man standing on the porch in front of her. He was wearing a ski mask.

The last thing she saw was the sawed-off shotgun in his hands.

CHAPTER NINETEEN

BLAM!!!

Charlie jumped. "*Jesus!*" he shouted.

He'd been about to round the corner into the entry hall when he heard the shotgun blast. Something moist splattered onto his face, as a human form was propelled past him into the living room.

Back by the kitchen, Odif gave out with a frightened yelp.

Charlie felt disoriented. It was like he was in a dream, not quite sure what was happening or where he was.

He stared at the shredded heap of crimson stained denim that had rebounded off the back of the sofa onto the floor. He knew that was Brenda. It had to be her. But, her face was gone, and....

He wiped his cheek and came up with blood on his hand. "Oh, God!" he said to himself. "*Oh, my God!*"

He heard the click of metal to his right. Glancing around the corner into the entry, he saw the two men. Both wore ski masks and down jackets. The largest of the pair had just broken open his double-barreled shotgun and was replacing the shells. The other, much shorter but almost as stocky, was brandishing a .44 Magnum.

The short gunman spotted Charlie. Grasping the .44 with both hands, he brought the weapon up to fire.

Charlie saw the gunman aim the Magnum at him. Inside, his gut shouted, "*Move*, shmuck!"

Charlie dove sideways and hit the ground.

BLAM!!!

The slug blasted a fist-sized hole in the wall where he'd been standing.

He scrambled back into the kitchen on his hands and knees. Odif growled.

Hearing the dog, the gunmen hesitated momentarily in the entry before proceeding forward.

Charlie crouched on the kitchen floor. His mind spun incessantly, as his eyes scanned the cramped room, seeking a way out.

The utensil drawer. There were knives in there. And one of them was a big mother that he'd bought because it reminded him of the one Anthony Perkins had used in *Psycho*.

He crept over to the drawer and opened it.

Again, Odif growled.

Moving out of the entry, the gunmen covered each other, as they proceeded slowly along opposite sides of the hallway toward the kitchen.

Charlie gripped the long knife. He wondered how he was going to use it against a double-barreled shotgun and a .44.

His attention focused on the coffee maker. It was perking. The brown liquid had to be boiling hot.

A plan began to formulate. It was a sensational plan, he thought. Right out of a Jason Bourne movie. Now, if only those bastards out there would just follow the script.

"What the fuck," Charlie reasoned, reaching up and grabbing the coffee carafe. "Being dead wasn't that bad." He just hoped that *dying* didn't hurt too much.

He moved over toward the kitchen entry where Odif had stationed himself, eyes wide open and ears perked up and listening. He set down the carafe and stroked the animal's coat.

Odif tensed and growled once more.

A light shadow moved on the hallway wall.

Charlie adjusted into a crouching position. The knife was in one hand and the carafe in the other. He took a deep breath. "You're Vin fucking Diesel," he told himself.

"Sic 'em, Odif!" he shouted. "*Sic 'em!*"

The Shepherd sprang around the corner and leapt on the hood carrying the shotgun. The man tumbled over backwards.   Odif was right on top of him, his sharp teeth ripping at his jacket.

BLAM!!!

One barrel of the weapon discharged wild, blasting a hole in the ceiling.

The shorter gunman aimed his .44 at the animal and pulled back the hammer.

Almost at the same instant, Charlie came barreling out of the kitchen. "*Grraagh!!*" he roared in his best Vin Diesel battle cry.   Startled, the hood turned the Magnum in his direction. Charlie let go with the contents of the carafe. The steaming coffee hit the man square in the face.

The gunman screamed and grabbed at his eyes. Holding the knife in front of him, Charlie smashed his full body weight into the hood. The blade sliced harmlessly through the outer edge of the down jacket. Both men went sprawling onto the floor. The knife slid across the hardwood and came to rest under a bookcase.

Charlie turned to shift back onto his feet, the carafe still in his hand. He found himself looking at Brenda's bloodied torso. He froze, as the ultimate truth of the situation flushed over him.

A few feet away, Odif ripped at his adversary's mask. The man, kicking and using one arm, tried to push the growling beast away. With his free hand, he maneuvered the shotgun toward the animal's belly.

BLAM!!!

Odif yelped. The bits of his bloodied carcass smashed against the hallway wall.

The blast shook Charlie back to reality. He scrambled to his feet. He saw that the hood who had just killed his dog was also getting up, and that his partner appeared to be recovering from any damage done by the coffee.

Charlie glanced at the front door. It was still open. He figured he had maybe two seconds to get through it.

He hurled the carafe at the hood with the .44. The container smashed onto the wall next to the man, shattering glass over his mask.

"*Shit!*" the hood cried out, grabbing at his head.

Charlie bolted toward the door. His foot slipped on the wood, but he regained his balance without falling.

His weapon empty, the hood with the shotgun snatched up his partner's .44 and fired a quick shot after his intended victim.

The slug splintered the door arch, just as Charlie raced through the opening.

"Come on," the hood said, helping his disabled partner to his feet. "We can't let 'im get away."

Charlie tore out of the house and headed toward his Mercedes. Halfway there, he stopped. The car would be of no help. A dark blue Buick was blocking it in the driveway.

He dashed down to the street and, crossing the short cul-de-sac, looked in every direction for people.

People would mean safety. So would just a single person. A passing car. A neighbor's house with a friendly light in the window. The street was empty and dark except for a lone lamp on the corner.

This had always been a quiet street. Privacy was why he'd originally moved here. He'd liked these houses, hidden atop high ivy-covered grades and protected by long driveways, walls of carved stone and electric gates. He never saw or knew his neighbors, and they never saw or knew him.

"I should move to a friendlier neighborhood and learn to be more sociable," he thought to himself, the final scene from *It's a Wonderful Life* flashing through his head. "Could I use Jimmy Stewart's neighbors now."

Careful to stay out of the lamp's glow, Charlie sprinted toward the corner and Mulholland Drive. There'd be traffic there. Hopefully, somebody would stop for him.

"*There he goes!*" a man shouted behind him. He didn't have to turn around to know who was speaking. As he reached Mulholland, he heard the car engine start.

Mulholland was empty. There were no vehicles coming from either direction. He glanced at his watch. It read ten after eight.

"Where the fuck *is* everybody!" he shouted, heading west toward Laurel.

Running along the winding road, Charlie felt like a frightened animal trapped in some sort of laboratory maze. To his left, a steep wall of rock rose up to the top of the hill, while his other side was bordered by a brush covered embankment that dropped down to the valley below.

Beyond that, miles away, the bright lights of the San Fernando Valley stretched before him in a panoramic view.

He heard the screech of rubber on pavement. He knew that was the Buick, maybe a block or so behind him. He wasn't about to glance back to see just how far.

Rounding a curve, he spotted a pair of headlights up ahead. They were moving toward him fast.

"I'm gonna stop this son-of-a-bitch," he thought, running toward the oncoming vehicle. He began to wave his arms.

"*Stop!*" he shouted. "*Help me!*"

He was answered by the beeping of the horn, as the red MG swerved to miss him. "*Asshole!*" the young driver called, then he accelerated and disappeared around the bend.

Charlie screamed a frustrated "*Fuck you!*" and flashed his middle finger. He heard the horn beep again, followed by another screech of the tires.

The Buick now tore around the curve and headed straight toward him. "*Shit!*" Charlie yelled, as he turned and resumed his flight west. He could feel the vehicle drawing closer, its headlights illuminating the road ahead.

BLAM!!!

Something ricocheted off the pavement next to him. "Jesus," he thought, "they're shooting at me." He strained to increase his speed, but he knew that his endurance was beginning to wane.

Without slowing, he glanced over his shoulder. The Buick was almost on top of him. The hood on the passenger side, his head and arm out the window, was taking aim with the Magnum.

BLAM!!!

Charlie heard the slug whistle past his ear. He knew he had to get off the road... *now*, or he'd be dead within seconds.

His gut told him there was only one thing he could do. He had no time to think about it. No time to contemplate the consequences.

He dashed over to the cliff side of the road. The Buick bore down for the coup de grâce. "*Fuck you, cocksuckers!*" Charlie shouted, as he leaped over the embankment.

The driver of the Buick slammed on the brakes. He tried to swerve the vehicle away from the cliff. Too late. The car skidded and the right front tire, then the right rear went over.

"*Shit!*" Charlie's right ankle twisted when it hit the side of the embankment. He pitched forward and started to roll, the brush and rocks tearing at his clothing and skin. He reached out and grabbed at a shrub, but the plant pulled out by its roots. He continued his fall.

Above him, the Buick careened over the side of the road and began to roll down the embankment. The men inside screamed, as their vehicle plunged past Charlie.

Near the base of the hill, the back end of the car bounced off a boulder, exploding the gas tank. In seconds, the car was engulfed in flames. The screams inside were now reflecting both terror *and* pain.

Charlie slid into some bushes...prickly bushes...and stopped falling. He felt like he'd been through a slicing machine. But, there wasn't time to examine his wounds. The car had set the dry scrub brush covered hill ablaze, and the inferno was heading in his direction.

He struggled out of the bushes and managed to get to his feet. A sharp pain shot through his foot then came back and stayed in his right ankle. He shifted his weight and stumbled down toward the bottom of hill.

Ahead, he could see a street and houses.

CHAPTER TWENTY

Jenny signed the receipt and accepted the large envelope from the clerk. She'd never received Express Mail before. Finding the notice in her mailbox that afternoon had surprised her. "Who sent it?" she'd wondered, as she'd hurried over to the post office to find out.

Even before the envelope was in her hands, she'd "known" that it was from Charlie. Nobody else in her life would go to that trouble or expense. Lawyers and businessmen called long distance or sent registered letters. She'd learned all about that when her father's estate was probated.

"Charlie's probably come up with some cute and elaborate explanation," she'd thought, as she'd waited in line at the window. "That's his style." The idea of Express Mail *was* flattering to her ego. But underneath, she wasn't quite sure anymore how she felt about the relationship.

"Excuse me," she corrected herself. "'Affair'."

Her impromptu phone call to Los Angeles the night before last had shaken her. She knew that Charlie had secrets. Every guy had secrets. But, like a dope, she'd *believed* him when he'd told her that he was crazy about her and wanted to be with her.

"Hell," she thought, "what he wants is to be with me in Dallas, and with that Brenda person in California."

Anxious to inspect its contents, she carried the envelope over to the desk against the wall and started to open it. Then, she noticed the tall black man in the beige suit who'd parked in the post office lot just after she'd pulled in. He was standing by the stamp machine, and he appeared to be watching her out of the corner of his eye. His presence made her uneasy. She decided to head for home and read the letter there.

"Damn Charlie!" she said to herself, as she climbed into her Volvo. He'd even started her daydreaming again about "living happily ever after". That was the kind of rubbish that had gotten her into trouble before.

"Expectations can be dangerous," Dr. Perryman had told her. She'd gone to him for a few sessions after her father died, when she'd broken up with Danny.

She maneuvered her car out of her parking space and headed it for the street. Through her rearview mirror, she saw the tall black man in the beige suit come out of the building and head for his vehicle. "I'm getting paranoid," she told herself, as she cut in front of a gray Nisian so that she could lose herself in traffic.

She hadn't seen Danny for just over a year now. He was also a teacher, and a home computer enthusiast. They'd met at an educator's luncheon. He was a quiet, sensitive fellow, who wore glasses and sported a cute crewcut. She'd been dating him only a few weeks when her father had suffered his stroke and left her alone.

But Danny, like her father when he was alive, had been there for her. He'd seen her through those difficult months of dealing with the funeral home, attorneys and, especially, the loneliness.

She'd come to depend on him, and she'd fallen in love. She'd assumed that he loved her, too.

"Never *assume* anything," Dr. Perryman had said. "You'll only get yourself into bad trouble that way."

She'd learned that for herself when, after a particularly marvelous lovemaking session, she'd dared to mention that terrible word, "marriage". Danny had tensed and shifted toward the other side of the bed. "I'm not ready for that," he'd said.

They'd seen each other less and less after that night. He was developing a new game for the computer that he claimed could make him millions. "I've gotta finish this," he'd told her. And they'd just drifted apart.

"Why are all men flakes?" she asked herself. "Correction: Why do *I* always *fall* for flakes?"

She was still mulling that question when she entered her apartment. She tossed the envelope onto the kitchen table. "Better relax for this one," she said, pouring herself a glass of Chablis.

The packet contained a dozen or so handwritten pages. All but the top two sheets were photocopies. Jenny looked at the originals first.

Dear Jenny,

When you read this, I may be dead.

I know that sounds very dramatic, but a lot has happened during the last few hours.

I really screwed up this time. You may read about it in the papers, or hear about it on the radio or TV. They'll probably say that I'm a crook, which is true. They might also say that I'm a murderer, which is not true.

The truth, as <u>I</u> know it, is in the enclosed Xerox pages. This whole thing began with my out-of-body experience, and I've written down everything I've done since then. It's a fantastic story, yet you of all people should believe it. I've sent the original to my lawyer in Los Angeles. His name is Miles Goodman, and I've given him your name and number.

You can trust Miles.

Jenny, I didn't lie to you about my feelings. But, when I met you, I wasn't living in a vacuum. There were old entanglements to end, and I was trying to do that in a way that wouldn't hurt (or at least not hurt too badly) somebody who has been very important in my life. That was Brenda. She's gone now.

If I get out of this thing, which is highly unlikely, maybe we can talk. I love you very, very much, and I do want to try to put us back together again.

If I don't make it, please do me the favor of contacting Miles. Maybe, between the two of you, you can get my story told.

I'd hate to see those bastards get away with it.

Be well, Jenny. You mean a lot to me.

Charlie

Jenny finished the letter and wiped the tears from her eyes. She poured herself another Chablis, then turned to the photocopied pages.

What she read was an analytical day-by-day, detailed account of Charlie's investigation and plight, beginning with the automobile accident and his subsequent out-of-body experience; through his inquiries in Dallas, Los Angeles and Muni; his meeting with Moreno's son; the faux pas at the political meeting; and his recent arrest for violations of the Federal copyright law. By the time she'd reached the section describing Brenda's slaying, Jenny was weeping again. "Oh, Charlie," she said, trying to digest what she'd just learned, "what have you gotten yourself into?"

She looked back at the papers in her hand and noted that there was one final page that she hadn't read.

I'm all alone in this.

I may have gotten rid of those two guys they sent after me, but there'll be others. They have to kill me now, because they think I know too much.

If I go to the police, they won't believe me and I'll be arrested for Brenda's murder.

That'll give Harlow and company a perfect shot at me. He has friends in high places.

I guess I'm going to have to handle this one myself.

Charles Powers

Jenny set down the pages. She felt she had to do *something*...call *somebody*, but she didn't know *who* that should be. She started to take a sip of wine and realized that her hands were trembling. "Okay! Okay!" she said to herself. "Just relax. Think it out."

The knock on the door made her jump. For a moment, she considered not responding. "Who is it?" she said finally.

There was no response.

She tiptoed to the door and peeked through the peephole. "Oh, God!" she muttered, seeing the black man in the beige suit standing outside her apartment door. She was thinking of hiding somewhere, when he knocked again.

"Miss Bradshaw," the man called. "I'm from the F.B.I. I know you're in there."

"Do you have identification?" Jenny asked, without touching the door.

The man held his I.D. up to the peephole. Jenny thought it looked official. She unlocked the door and opened it. "Why have you been following me?" she demanded.

Agent Billy Lee Davis flashed a friendly smile, as he stepped into the apartment. "We're looking for Charlie Powers," he said, glancing around the room. "We understand from the people at Parkland Hospital that the two of you became pretty friendly while he was a patient there."

"Why do you want him?"

"He's under a Federal indictment, and he's disappeared." Davis started to move further into the apartment. With a surge of bravado, Jenny blocked his path.

The agent took a step backwards and shook his head. "He's also wanted for questioning by the Los Angeles authorities on a murder charge."

"How do you know he did it?"

"I don't know anything, Miss Bradshaw," he said, exhibiting his smile again. "All I'm trying to do is find him."

"He's not here," Jenny snapped. "And you can't search without a warrant."

"I can get one of those. But I thought we could do this the easy way. If you cooperate with me, maybe I can help you and help him, too."

"I don't know where he is."

Davis raised an eyebrow. "Didn't he tell you in that Express Mail packet you just picked up?"

Jenny studied Billy Lee's hazel eyes. He was a smart one all right, but there was something about him she trusted. She *had* to trust somebody. "If I help you," she said, "what are you going to do to Charlie?"

"Depends on what he's done."

"*I* believe his story."

"Well, maybe if you give me a chance, I'll believe it, too."

"I doubt it," she said, walking back into the kitchen. She handed Davis the photocopied pages. "You want some wine?" she asked, pouring herself another glass.

"No, thank you." Davis scanned the pages, as if he'd taken a speed-reading class. "Miss Bradshaw," he said when he'd finished, "this is pure... speculation."

"I knew you'd say that."

"This out-of-body experience stuff...."

"My father had an out-of-body experience," Jenny interrupted, "and *I* saw him."

"That may be, Miss Bradshaw" Davis said, endeavoring politeness. "I know there are some scientists who believe in that....theory." He set the pages back onto the table. "But, the fact remains that there's nothing in these papers that could be called evidence. Nothing at all."

"What about those two men who killed...Brenda?"

"It's a local matter. The Los Angeles authorities will investigate."

"You're not the least bit interested, are you?" Jenny turned away to hide her new flood of tears.

"The F.B.I. has no authority in this murder case. We just want to make sure that Mr. Powers stands trial for his Federal offense."

She opened her mouth to use a word that, as a child, had earned her a meal of soapsuds. The ringing of phone stopped her. "Hello," she said, grateful for the intrusion.

"Miss Bradshaw?"

"Yes?"

"This is Miles Goodman. Do you know who I am?"

"I certainly do," Jenny grinned. She looked over at Davis and announced, "It's the cavalry."

CHAPTER TWENTY-ONE

The coffee had turned cold. He considered gulping it down to avoid the bitter taste, then decided he'd suffered enough these past three days. At the very least, he warranted a good cup of coffee. He motioned to the Mexican busboy who was clearing the next table.

"Fresh cup, please."

"Yes, mister." The young man hurried off to the bus stand to get the carafe.

Since the other night, Charlie'd been eating all his meals in this dingy little coffee shop with its lousy food and cracked plastic tabletops. He was tired of it. He was tired of the third-rate motel room that he'd been sleeping in. He was tired of running.

Yet, he felt relatively safe. Nobody would look for him in Sunland. Nobody he knew ever went that far north. He figured that two thirds of the people in Los Angeles didn't even know the small community was in the San Fernando Valley. He'd only discovered it because he'd once attended a party out there. And, he'd gotten lost looking for the address.

He glanced at his watch, then looked over at the wall phone. "Where the fuck are they?" he pondered. He decided he'd give them another fifteen minutes, then forget about it for tonight.

A slight young man in a hot pink jacket slid into the next booth. Charlie couldn't help smirking at the guy's frosted hair and mascara. He wondered why the guy was way out here in the sticks, and not on the Sunset Strip where his type belonged.

He turned and looked back out the window. He'd been looking out of windows quite a bit lately. He could see the images much more clearly that way. And, the images never changed. They were like short little clips of film that kept replaying in his mind's eye.

They always began the same way. A shotgun blast would echo through his head, followed by that red-hued picture of Brenda's shattered body flying backwards into the living room.

Cut. Another shotgun blast, and Odif's insides were pasted onto the hallway walls.

Cut. He'd be racing down Mulholland Drive, the Buick bearing down on him. Closer...closer, until he could almost feel the heat from its engine.

Cut. Over the cliff he'd leap, rolling down the canyon side, rocks and bushes ripping at his body, as the exploding vehicle plunged toward him.

"You okay, mister?"

The images dissolved quickly into the present. Charlie pulled a flimsy paper napkin out of the metal holder and wiped the perspiration from his forehead.

"Here's your coffee, mister." Carafe in hand, the smiling busboy stood by the table, waiting for Charlie to acknowledge the fresh brew.

Charlie took a sip from the cup. The stuff tasted just as bad as the last batch. "It's okay," he nodded, anxious for the man to leave. "Thank you."

"Thank you, mister." The busboy seemed pleased as he walked away.

Charlie looked out the window again. He didn't want to lose those images. Their memory would help him accomplish what he knew he had to do.

He marveled at how he'd survived that night. Dazed, bleeding and with clothing torn, he'd walked over two miles down the dark canyon roads to Ventura Boulevard. In a corner Seven-Eleven, he'd purchased some bandages, gauze, antiseptic and a six-pack of Coors.

"You look like you had an accident," the cashier commented.

Charlie hadn't answered. He'd just walked out of the store and checked into an adult-oriented motel across the street. The desk clerk had eyed him carefully through the bulletproof glass in the check-in window. "You okay?" he'd asked.

"Yeah," Charlie had said, trudging off to his room.

Without turning on the light, he'd locked the door behind him, found the bed and collapsed. He had no idea how long he slept. It was the piercing siren, wailing down Ventura Boulevard that woke him.

He'd bolted upright on the bed. Drenched with perspiration and his body aching from his wounds, he'd dashed to the window to see what had happened. He began to realize...to remember where he was. It was then that the images had first come.

He'd felt sick. He knew he was going to vomit. In the dim light, he could make out the open bathroom door. He'd hurried over and emptied his guts into the toilet bowl.

Later, as he'd lay soaking away his physical pains in the double-sized heart-shaped bathtub, the truth of his situation began to weigh on him. "Brenda," he said aloud, feeling her loss. The tears started to come and they didn't stop.

"In the Hollywood Hills tonight, police are investigating the murder of a yet unidentified woman killed by a shotgun blast."

Charlie had been in the bathroom, trying to wrap a bandage around his forearm, when he heard the newscaster. He stepped into the bedroom and looked at the television screen. "That's *my* place," he'd thought, as he watched the tape of the police milling around the outside of his house.

The newscaster had continued: "There are no clues yet in this bizarre case, although authorities are seeking for questioning one Charles Powers, who has been leasing the house."

Charlie's mug shot flashed onto the screen. "Shit!" he muttered. "I'm a regular John Dillinger."

"Powers is currently under Federal indictment for various violations of the copyright laws." The tape revealed two men from the coroner's office carrying a black body bag out of the house.

Tears began to form in Charlie's eyes again, as he'd watched the body being placed into the ambulance. "Brenda," he cried, "I'm so sorry."

The next item on the newscast had jostled Charlie out of his weeping. "About a mile away from the murder scene," said the newscaster, "a major brush fire is blazing in the rugged hillside along Mulholland Drive." Taped footage of firefighters struggling to subdue the flames flashed onto the screen. "The cause of the inferno was a tragic automobile accident, which took the lives of two men."

Staring at the television, the melancholy passed from Charlie. It was replaced by anger. "*Fuck them!*" he said to himself. "*Burn in hell!*" He felt his gut harden, as the scenario for his revenge took shape in his mind.

He knew he had to get to Harlow. That was the only way. Expose him or kill him, it made no difference. He was going to destroy the son-of-a-bitch. And, if he went down in the process, then...what the fuck, his life was shit anyway.

He took a bite off a fingernail, then pulled the tab off one of the Coors and gulped down half the can. "Of course," he'd thought, "if I'm smart, I'll get Harlow and walk away from this thing scot-free."

"Julius!" Charlie berated himself for not thinking of him before. Julius was a film buff who bought pirated DVDs from Charlie. He was also a hustler and a pimp, but he'd been working the street for most of his fifty years, and he had connections, sources of information.

"If only I'd gone to him yesterday...." He had refused to dwell on the rest of that thought. "I'll go see him tomorrow," he decided.

The money in his bankroll totaled $587.00 plus a Visa card. He'd always carried a large wad because, in an underground business like film piracy, cash talked. If he was careful, there would be enough to do the job.

He'd spent the next three hours writing his "just in case" letter to Miles and Jenny. If anything went wrong with his plan, he knew he could count on one, if not both of them, to do "something" with that information.

Next morning, he'd photocopied and mailed the letters. Jenny's copy was sent Express Mail and Miles' went certified. Then, after buying some fresh shirts, jeans and a sports coat, he'd rented a gray Mustang from Avis.

"When'll you have it back?" the clerk had asked, as she'd embossed Charlie's Visa card onto the rental forms.

"Within a week."

On his way out to Sunland, he'd driven up Sepulveda Boulevard and stopped at the Bright Lights, a strip joint in Panorama City. The front door was locked. He stepped back, surveying the building's facade of peeling pink paint and graffiti obscenities. Had the place gone out of business, he'd wondered. He knocked on the box-office window.

"We're not open yet," the golden-haired black chick said, as she'd stuck her head into the box-office.

"I want to see Julius."

"He's not here."

"Don't worry, honey," Charlie assured her. "I'm not a cop."

"I know you're not them," she snapped. "They already raided the place last night."

Charlie resisted the temptation to quip, "What *else* is new?" Instead he said, "He doesn't owe me any money. Just tell him that Charlie's here?"

The girl glowered at him. "I told ya, he's not around."

"Let Julius decide that."

Her head had disappeared from the box-office, and he heard her say, "It's some honky dude. Calls hisself Charlie'."

The front door of Bright Lights opened. "Hey!" Julius had grinned, flaunting the diamond chip embedded in his front tooth, "It's the man with the movies."

Charlie had looked up at the black man in the Hawaiian shirt and returned the smile. "How's it goin'?" They'd shook hands like "brothers". He noticed the new four-carat diamond on Julius' large finger. "Must be goin' good," he said, answering his own question.

"For a guy who's just spent the night in jail, I guess I'm well enough."

"What happened?"

"Same ol' thing. The vice guys claimed that one of my gals was up on stage playing with her pussy too much."

"Was she?"

"No more than the usual," Julius had cackled. "Come on in. I'll buy you a beer."

Charlie stepped into the building. The place was dark, except for a work light in the foyer that illuminated the worn carpet and its collection of the previous night's litter. The chick with the golden hair stood behind the inside box-office counter, looking annoyed and filing her nails. Charlie smiled at her and pointed to Julius. "I guess he just came in, huh?"

"Hey, girl," Julius had said. "That vacuum in the closet still needs somebody to push it."

"I'm gettin' to it," she'd snapped.

"What do you got that's good these days?" Julius asked, leading Charlie through the cabaret section of the structure. "You know, my friends still can't believe I was showin' Denzel's last flick on my TV before it was in the theaters."

In the blackness, Charlie had nearly tripped over one of the chairs. "I'm buying today," he said, "not selling." He felt for the edge of the stage to guide him across the room. Julius opened the office door at the far end of the cabaret. Charlie headed for the light.

The office was simple in its furnishings: a scratched metal desk, two scratched metal chairs and a scratched metal filing cabinet. Wall decor was cheesecake, courtesy of *Playboy* and *Hustler*.

"Been seein' yer picture in the paper," Julius said, grabbing two beers from a cooler behind the desk.

"Forget that," Charlie said. "I need a gun." He pulled his bankroll out of his pocket.

"Figured that's what you wanted."

"*Now*."

"No sweat." Julius peeled down the tape that was holding Miss July onto the wall. The foldout had been covering a hole in the plaster. "The cops never look behind my art collection." He'd reached into the hole and withdrawn a *Star Wars* lunch pail. "My kids always liked that Darth Vader."

"You got an automatic?"

"I just got this one piece now." Julius opened up the pail and took out a revolver. "It's a .38 Rossi. Made in Brazil."

"It only holds five rounds," Charlie had said, as he examined the weapon.

Julius cackled again. "But I got hollow-tipped bullets for ya." He'd pulled a box of ammunition out of the pail. "So, you're only gonna have to hit the sucker once."

"How much?"

"Two bucks."

———

"That's pretty steep."

"You're pretty hot."

Charlie had pared two one hundred dollar bills off his bankroll and handed them to Julius. There were fifty shells in the box. He loaded five into the Rossi, and then stuck the gun into his belt.

"You want to shoot your dick off?" Julius had asked. He reached into the wall hole again and came out with a calf holster. "Here's a present for ya."

"Thanks," Charlie said, kneeling to strap it on.

"No sweat." Julius sat down and put his feet up on the desk. "There's some people lookin' for you, you know."

"What kind of people?"

"People from Texas."

Charlie had leaned against the wall and sipped his beer. "I was thinking of calling them," he said.

The coffee was cold again. Charlie looked at his watch. It had been almost a half-hour since he'd set his fifteen-minute deadline. He figured that they weren't going to phone tonight. He wondered if they were going to call at all.

"Hi!" In the next booth, the guy with the hot pink jacket smiled as Charlie passed by on his way to the cash register.

Charlie ignored him. He was debating what his next move would be if they didn't call. "Maybe I'll go to another political meeting," he mused. "I could jump up on the stage and put a gun to Harlow's head." He smiled at the idea. "That should make the S.W.A.T. team happy."

He'd just finished paying his check when the wall phone rang.

"Biltmore Coffee Shop," the Mexican busboy answered. Charlie was halfway to the phone, as the busboy replied, "We don't got no Charlie Powers here, mister."

"Hold it!" Charlie said, grabbing the receiver, "that's me."

"How'm I suppose to know that, mister?" the busboy muttered, returning to his duties.

"This is Powers," Charlie said into the phone.

"We've got his schedule." The male monotone reflected only the slightest hint of a Texas drawl.

Charlie thought he felt his heart skip a beat. "Good."

"You know the outdoor newsstand at Ventura and Van Nuys?"

"Yeah."

"Pick you up at eleven."

Charlie hung up the receiver and beamed. "I did it!" he thought to himself, as he danced out of the coffee shop and headed for the Mustang. "It's going to happen."

He was unlocking the car door when his gut started speaking to him again. For a few moments, he didn't move. He chewed on his thumbnail, as he tried to sort his thoughts.

They were going along with him. That made him happy. On the other hand, he'd never made a deal with the devil before, and that scared the shit out of him.

CHAPTER TWENTY-TWO

Charlie stepped out of the corner phone booth and walked over to the newsstand. He kept questioning himself whether his last minute phone call had been a smart move. Insurance like that could be expensive, especially if things didn't go exactly as planned.

He buried his face in a copy of *Entertainment Weekly*, as the black-and-white proceeded down Van Nuys Boulevard and turned right onto Ventura.

"That's all I need," he thought. "To get spotted by some hotshot cop when I'm this close."

Putting the magazine back into the rack, he strolled along the half block, perusing the glut of books and periodicals. His attention zeroed in on a headline in the *Daily News*: "Shotgun Victim Identified As Actress." Next to the story was his mug shot, featuring the caption, "Boyfriend Sought."

"Old news." Charlie dismissed the newspaper as being too depressing, then checked his watch and peered down Van Nuys Boulevard. He took a bite off of what was left of his fingernails and wondered why Moreno was always late.

Yesterday, after he'd found his out-of-the-way motel in Sunland and set-up an "office" at the Biltmore Coffee Shop, Charlie had used the wall phone to call the junior Godfather in Dallas. "He's not here," a reedy male voice had informed him.

"Tell him that his friend from the airport tram wants a meeting," Charlie had said.

"Who is this?"

"Tell him to meet me tomorrow night at the Denny's restaurant in Van Nuys. Ten o'clock."

The next evening, Charlie had made certain that he arrived at Denny's by nine-thirty. He'd checked out the faces of the half-dozen customers in the place and decided that they were probably okay. None of them looked like Mafia hit men.

"What does a Mafia hit man look like?" he'd laughed to himself. "For all I know that little old lady over there has a .44 Magnum and two grenades in her purse."

He'd sat himself in a corner booth near the kitchen, his back to the wall. He knew that the rear door was through the kitchen, should he be forced to make a quick exit. He placed the Rossi on the seat next to him, ordered a cup of coffee and waited. After a few minutes, he began humming the *Raider's* march.

At five-after-ten, he had started thinking that Moreno was having trouble finding the coffee shop.

At ten-after-ten, he'd started considering the possibility that Moreno hadn't received his message.

At a quarter after, he was irked and about to write the evening off as a total bust, when he'd caught sight of two expensive western-style suits entering the restaurant. He motioned Moreno and his big pal, Eddie, over to the booth.

"Hear you been lookin' for me," Charlie had said. He indicated that the men should sit across from him. Eddie remained standing.

Moreno slid in next to the wall. "I don't think we're the only ones."

"I'm very popular," Charlie quipped. He finished off his coffee. "What do you want?"

"Games *again*, Mr. Powers?" Moreno had sighed and laughed the icy little chuckle that Charlie remembered from their last confrontation. "In Dallas, I gave you the benefit of the doubt, but this time...." He had shrugged and gestured to Eddie. The large man grinned, cracked his knuckles and took a step forward.

"*Sit*, Eddie!" Charlie had snapped, snatching up the Rossi and leveling under the table at the henchman. "Sit, or I'll shoot your balls off."

Eddie had hesitated. Moreno held up his hands in a mock gesture of surrender. He motioned to Eddie to sit at the next table. "You've...changed," he'd said to Charlie.

"Let's say, I've stopped laughing." He put the weapon back on the seat next to him.

"You've 'what'?"

"Private joke." He studied Moreno for a few moments, wondering if he could really trust him. Then, he'd decided that, at this point, he had no choice. "I've got the name you want," he said. "But, you already know that, don't you?"

"Our sources in Phoenix said there was a contract out on you. You had to be close to something."

"*Too* close."

"What's your price?"

"Fifty grand and a way out of the country."

"No problem."

"And I want in on the kill."

Moreno appeared mildly amused. Again, he'd emitted his icy little chuckle.

This time, Charlie chuckled back. "I'd do it myself," he'd continued, "but I figure you can get to him easier than me."

"Okay," Moreno had agreed. "Done. Who is he?"

Charlie gave him Harlow's name.

"Isn't he a pretty big wheel out here?"

"Could be our next governor."

"Are you sure he's the one?"

Charlie had found the Texan's deadpan reaction to be a bit unsettling. "I'm sure," he said. "*You* don't seem that surprised."

"Stranger things have happened."

"Like out-of-body experiences?"

"I'll assume you've done your homework," Moreno nodded. "Do you know where he lives?"

"Bel Air."

Moreno gestured toward Eddie. "Give him a number where we can reach you the next couple of nights."

"He's a cool one" Charlie had thought, watching Moreno slide out of the booth and exit the restaurant. He scribbled out the phone number of the Biltmore on the back of a paper napkin and handed it to Eddie.

"Be seein' ya," the big man smiled, and then he'd followed his boss out.

"Hello, killer." Moreno smiled from the rear seat of the vehicle that had just pulled up next to the newsstand. "Get in."

Charlie found it difficult to hide his astonishment. He stuck the copy of *Entrepreneur* back onto the rack and walked to the curb. "We're going to do this in a *black limousine*?" he whispered.

"Limos are at Harlow's place every day. Nobody'll give it a second look."

Charlie sat down next to Moreno and shut the door. Eddie pulled the Cadillac away from the curb, and then made a U-turn, heading back toward the Freeway.

"I got a question." Charlie asked, as the vehicle changed from the Ventura Freeway onto the southbound San Diego. "How much *was* in that suitcase your father was carrying?"

"Three million. It was on its way to the laundry."

"And, with all your sources of information, you never knew about Harlow? He was never a suspect?

Moreno shrugged. "Nobody'd heard of him. He was clean."

"Then, how'd he know about the money?"

"That's what we'll find out tonight."

Charlie turned away and looked out the window. He could hear his gut debating. It was trying to figure if Moreno was planning to bump him off before or after he took care of Harlow.

The limo turned off the freeway at Sunset and headed for Bel Air's east gate. "What time does he get home?" Charlie asked.

"Around midnight," Moreno said. "He's out making a speech."

As Eddie maneuvered the car up around the winding roads of the exclusive community, Charlie took an extra look at an ivy-covered wall on St. Cloud Road. He knew that on the other side was the one-time residence of another of his idols, Carole Lombard. She'd lived there before her marriage to Clark Gable. Like the Lou Costello house, Charlie hoped to fake his way in there someday.

"Someday," he mumbled to himself.

Eddie took a left just south of the Bel Air Hotel and proceeded up another curve-ridden hill. He swung around a parked plumber's mini-van, then turned onto a short, secluded cul-de-sac.

"It's the end driveway," Moreno said, handing Eddie a small remote electronic control box. The henchman held the unit out his window, aiming it at the black metal post at the side of the driveway. The heavy wrought-iron gate slowly swung open.

"Where'd you get that?" Charlie asked.

"My nephew," Moreno said. "The kid's a genius. That device'll open any electronic gate you want."

The limo passed through the gate. The gate closed behind it.

"It's the servants' night off," Moreno said, as they proceeded up the lighted, tree-lined driveway. "We'll have the place to ourselves."

"How'd you pull that off?"

"Eddie can be very persuasive."

The Cadillac rounded a bend and Charlie spotted the majestic brick Tudor-style house, set in the center of what looked like a large rolling lawn. He imagined the place was built back in the twenties and probably had six bedrooms and the same number of baths. In the full moonlight, he caught a glimpse of the tennis court, swimming pool and cabaña to the rear of the property. "It's quite an estate," he said, wondering what silent film star had been the original owner.

Eddie turned into the circular driveway, and stopped in front of the main entrance. "We'll wait here," Moreno said, climbing out of the car. "Eddie'll hide the car, then let us in."

Charlie watched the limo disappear around the side of the house. "How's Eddie going to get in?" he asked, noting that the front porch light was on, as were some lamps inside the house.

"Planning," Moreno replied.

Two minutes later, Charlie heard glass break in the back of the house. "Great 'planning'," he said with a smirk, visualizing Eddie breaking a window.

Moreno offered his icy chuckle.

Eddie opened the front door and admitted the two men. "The key didn't work," he said, showing Moreno a bloodstained handkerchief wrapped around his left hand.

The house was as Charlie had imagined. It featured a large tiled entry, paneled in dark oak, with a long staircase leading up to the second floor. Fine paintings and art objects suggested an interest in western Americana. Charlie noted that two of the original pieces were, in fact, by Remington.

The living room was dark, except for a dim light that peeked out from what looked to be the den. Open curtains along the rear wall revealed a row of French doors leading out to the lawn.

"He's going to be a good half hour yet," Moreno said, looking at his watch. He turned to Eddie. "You didn't happen to see a bar on your way in, did you?"

"It's over here." The large man led the way into the den. He pushed shut the French patio door with the broken windowpane, and kicked the broken pieces of glass behind the leather sofa.

"Eddie's very neat." Moreno scooted behind the well-stocked oak bar and grabbed a bottle of Scotch. "Drink, Powers?"

"A short one." Charlie found himself scanning two floor-to-ceiling walls of books, with titles like, Winston Churchill's *The Second World War*, *The Complete Works of George Bernard Shaw* and a set of *The Great Books*. There were also complete collections from Time-Life Books: *The Old West*, *Human Behavior* and *Great Ages of Man*. "You think Harlow's read all these?" he asked. "Or, are they just there for show?"

"I don't think he went to college," Moreno said. He handed Charlie a half-filled highball glass. "To get from country boy to this place, he'd have to do a lot of self-educatin'."

"I'm impressed," Charlie said, thumbing through an *Old West* volume, entitled *The End of the Myth*.

The three men reacted to the slamming of a car door out front. "He's early," Moreno said. Eddie switched off the den light.

"More great planning?" Charlie asked.

"Does it really make a difference?" Moreno headed for the French doors. "We'll keep out of sight."

"*What!?!*" Charlie watched his two companions step out onto the patio.

"He might tell you more than us."

Before Charlie could protest further, Eddie had shut the patio door and disappeared with his boss into the darkness.

Out in the entry hall, the front door opened.

Charlie hadn't bargained for this. Confronting Harlow alone was not in his script. He tried to figure why Moreno was staying in the background. After all, it had been *his* father who'd been murdered. His gut screamed at him to get the hell out of there. But, unfortunately, there was no place to run.

"Shit," he muttered, as he knelt down and took the Rossi out of his calf holster. The weapon fumbled from his moist hand onto the floor. He wiped his palm on the leg of his jeans, then gripped the revolver and moved slowly toward the living room.

Somebody was approaching. He ducked behind the den door and held his breath.

Robert Harlow entered the room, switching on the light. Dressed in a gray pinstripe with collar unbuttoned and tie askew, the candidate appeared somewhat weary from a hard day of campaigning. He started behind the bar to pour himself a drink.

Charlie tried to think Robert DeNiro. "Turn around slow," he said, stepping out from behind the door.

The candidate did a slow spin. "Hello, Powers." He flashed a friendly smile and pointed at the Rossi. "Be careful that doesn't go off."

Charlie kept the revolver leveled at him. "You're not surprised to see me?" he said, trying to fathom the man's reaction.

"I knew you'd show up, sooner or later," Harlow said, sitting down onto a barstool. "Actually, I was looking forward to this meeting. I'm fascinated by this out-of-body stuff. At first, I thought...."

He stood up and started to move behind the bar again. "Do you mind if we have a drink? I've been speakin' all night, and I'm as dry as a prairie fire." He raised his right hand and crossed his heart with his left. "I promise I won't try a thing."

Charlie didn't speak, as Harlow started mixing two drinks. He was still trying to figure out what the hell was going on here.

———

219

"Anyway," Harlow continued, "at first I thought what you were spoutin' was pure bull crap. But, then I had to ask myself, 'how else would this boy know what he knows if he *hadn't* had some sort of psychic experience'?" He took a sip from his drink, and then winked at Charlie. "I mean, I am truly amazed."

"Stay there," Charlie ordered, as Harlow started around the bar to hand him his drink.

"It's good Scotch."

"I've already had some."

"Okay," Harlow shrugged.

"How'd you know about the three million?"

Harlow didn't answer. He simply smiled and started to laugh to himself.

"*I* told him," Moreno said, entering from the patio. Behind him, Eddie was aiming a .45 automatic at Charlie's gut.

Charlie felt the color drain from his face. His knees began to weaken.

"Toss the piece onto the chair," Eddie said.

Charlie obeyed. He looked over at Harlow, who was giving out with a loud, Texas-style guffaw. "Powers," the candidate beamed, "I don't know if I should say 'April Fool' or 'Trick or Treat'."

CHAPTER TWENTY-THREE

Jenny walked through the Delta gate and looked around the terminal for a pair of mutton chops.

"Miss Bradshaw?"

She threw a tentative smile at the man wearing the leather jacket and wire-frame spectacles. "Miles Goodman?"

"Nice to meet you." He reached for her overnight case. "Let me carry that."

"How did you recognize me?" she asked, as they headed for the escalators that descended to the street level.

"A lawyer's hunch," he said. "You look like your voice. Charlie has good taste."

"Thank you." She brushed a wisp of hair from her forehead. "Is there any news."

"None of it good. The police are watching Harlow...but, frankly, it's more of an effort to apprehend Charlie, rather than to investigate his story. They think he's going to try to kill Harlow."

"That worries me, too." They stepped off the escalator and started down the tunnel to the baggage claim area.

"I blame myself, in a way," Goodman said. "If I hadn't hung up on him the other day...."

"Mr. Goodman, if I hadn't had my own brush with out-of-body experience, I might not have believed Charlie either."

The lawyer's chuckle had a tinge of irony. "I still don't believe him," he said. "I just don't want anything bad to happen to him."

"Neither do I."

"*Counselor!*" The voice carried across the baggage claim area. Goodman did an about face. "We've been looking all over for you," Hal Stuart said, as he hurried over to them. "Your office told us you were down here."

"What's up?"

"Your client called me about an hour ago."

"Charlie?" Jenny interrupted.

Goodman made the introductions. "There was really no need for you to come to Los Angeles, Miss Bradshaw," Stuart said.

"I wanted to be here."

"What did Charlie say?" Goodman asked.

"Let's talk in the car." Stuart began escorting them toward the street.

"I have a suitcase," Jenny said.

Stuart motioned to a broad-shouldered fellow in a blue suit, who looked like he was a year out of law school. "Give me your claim check. I'll have Agent McNally bring it along."

"Stuart," Goodman demanded, "what's this all about?"

The agent stopped in the middle of the crosswalk and turned to Goodman. "We haven't got a lot of time, counselor. Now, if you want to prevent your client from being blown away by either Freddy Moreno or the L.A.P.D. S.W.A.T. team, you'd better come with me."

"Where are we going?" Jenny asked, as she tagged along toward the airport parking structure.

"Bel Air."

"I don't understand this," Charlie said, his moist hands gripping the arms of the leather chair. "I don't understand any of this."

Harlow handed Moreno a drink, then poured himself another. "Let me satisfy your curiosity," he said, lapsing into a touch of his native Texas drawl. "Freddy and I were drinking buddies back in Dallas. That was *before* he was a member of the 'organization'." He gestured a cocktail offer to Eddie who, .45 in hand, was leaning against the French doors, his gazed fixed on Charlie. The henchman shook his head.

"We both had big dreams," Harlow continued, sitting back on the barstool. "Dreams that needed money."

A picture of a gentle, wiry man in a pawnshop flipped through Charlie's mind. He looked over at Moreno. "You set up your own father?" he said, unable to conceal his contempt.

"He was a cold, cruel son-of-a-bitch." Moreno chewed at his lower lip.

"But, you were 'very close'," Charlie said with a smirk.

"He drove my mother to suicide."

Harlow laughed and took a sip from his glass. "Blood may be thicker than water," he said, "but three million bucks is three million bucks."

"Shut up, Bobby," Moreno snapped.

"That's not a nice way to talk to the next governor." Harlow's tone was taunting. He turned to Charlie. "Did you see today's polls?"

"In other words," Charlie said, "you get elected and, because there's no known link between the two of you...."

Harlow nodded. "You got the idea," he said. "A governor can grant a lot of favors." He cocked his head toward Moreno. "Right, partner?"

"Keep him talking," Charlie thought to himself. "Buy time. That's what James Bond would do." He glanced over at his Rossi, sitting on top of the bar where Eddie had set it.

He wondered how he was going to get his hands on it.

"Okay," Goodman said to Stuart, "before you kill us with your erratic driving, would you mind answering my question?"   He held onto the door armrest and braced his feet as the agent careened off of Century Boulevard and pointed the Ford sedan northward onto the San Diego Freeway. In the back seat, Jenny was also grasping for support. "What kind of deal did Charlie want to make with you?"

"He wanted immunity, in exchange for Freddy Moreno."

"That's not a bad offer," Goodman said.

"Particularly since he *says* he's going to deliver Moreno with a 'smoking gun' in his hand."

"How the hell is he going to do that."

"Maybe Moreno *believes* all that out-of-body bunk he's been spouting. Maybe Powers is going to get Moreno to blow Harlow away."

"And, you're going to let that happen?"

"How can I arrest somebody for a crime that hasn't taken place? Besides, murder is a local affair."

"I don't understand," Jenny said.

"It's a matter of jurisdiction." Goodman's answer had a tinge of sarcasm attached. "The F.B.I. is interested in Moreno and his cohorts because they're the Mafia...organized crime. They have no *official* interest in the murder of a local politician, even if he is running for governor." He turned back to Stuart. "You know that Moreno will never let Charlie witness that shooting and live, don't you?"

Stuart shook his head. "You got your head up your ass like most lawyers, counselor. I need your client as a witness. The L.A.P.D. aren't going to make a move against Harlow's house until they hear a gunshot. We're going to be on the scene to make sure their S.W.A.T. team gets there *in time*, and *doesn't* waste your precious Mr. Powers by mistake."

"Does that mean that you're going to give Charlie immunity?" Jenny asked.

"Lady," Stuart replied, "we want Moreno so bad that we'd be willing to give Hitler immunity."

"I doubt you'd go *that* far." Goodman winked at Jenny. She smiled back.

"*Damn it!*" Stuart said, spotting the road flares up ahead. He braked, bringing the sedan to a stop at the end of a forming line of vehicles. Behind him, other cars fell into the immobile procession, preventing any chance of backing up and turning around.

Goodman opened his door and stuck his head out. "There's an ambulance up there," he said. "It must be a bad one."

"Let me see what I can do." Pulling his identification wallet from his pocket, the agent got out of

the Ford and trotted up the freeway toward a Highway
Patrol car.

Charlie shifted his gaze to Eddie. The henchman
had relaxed his aim with the .45 and was now listening to
Harlow's pontificating on his achievement of success in
California business and politics.

"This is a funny state," the candidate said,
finishing his drink. "You have enough capital, and you
can accomplish anything you want in California." He
moved toward the end of the bar.

"Hell," Moreno retorted, "you have enough
capital, and you can accomplish anything you want
anywhere."

Harlow laughed again, then yawned. "You're
probably right, Freddy. But, I think it's more so here in
California."

Charlie looked back toward the bar. He estimated
that Harlow was about three feet from the Rossi. He
wondered if he should he make his move for the piece.
Maybe he *could* grab it before Eddie got off a shot.
Maybe he *could* be faster than a speeding bullet. Maybe
Superman man *would* arrive in the nick of time and save
his ass.

But, both George Reeves and Christopher Reeve
were dead and the new Superman was still making a
reputation for himself. So, if not the man of steel, then
maybe, at least, the F.B.I. would show up and save the
day.

He had to play for more time. "Why'd you keep
stringing me along?" he asked Harlow.

"You mean, why didn't Freddy take care of you
back in Dallas?"

"Something like that?"

"Good question," Harlow said. "You see, we didn't know *what* you knew, or *who* you'd been talkin' to. When you went into all that out-of-body stuff, we figured that nobody'd pay serious mind to you anyway...*unless* you turned up dead. Then, they just *might* start askin' around."

He replaced the liquor bottle back behind the bar. "Hell," he said, "if you hadn't shown up at that political meetin' out in the Valley, we probably would've let you be. You were just too dangerous after that."

Brenda's words of that fateful night did a quick replay through Charlie's brain. "I don't know *what* I believe," she'd said. "But, all of a sudden I'm very frightened to know you."

Charlie buried the painful memory. "But, why bring me here?" he persisted to Harlow. "Wouldn't it've been easier to have just bumped me off?"

"We tried that, as you know," the candidate answered with a chuckle. "Tonight, I must admit, was for my amusement. I mean, how can the spider resist a request from the fly to come into his parlor?" He glanced at his watch. "I've got speeches tomorrow," he said to Moreno. "It's past my bedtime."

"My amusement." Harlow's phrase stayed with Charlie. It grated like a fingernail on blackboard. The shotgun blast of the other night echoed in his head again, followed by that red-hued picture of Brenda's shattered body flying backwards into the living room.

"Fuck the F.B.I.!" Charlie thought, unleashing his anger. This *fucking son-of-a-bitch* is not going to get away with this." His attention shifted back to the Rossi.

Harlow rounded the bar, then strolled over and looked at the French doors. "Did you have to break the glass?" he scowled at Eddie.

"Didn't want him to get suspicious."

"Clean it up before you go." He started back across the room. "Freddy, would you please show our guest out?"

"Sure thing."

"*This is it!*" Charlie's gut warned. "Time's run out."

"Have another nice journey out-of-body, Mr. Powers." The politician guffawed at his own joke.

Charlie sprang to his feet as Harlow passed by him. He grabbed hold of the startled candidate, spinning him around. For a moment, Harlow was between him and Eddie.

The henchman's reaction was quick and instinctive. He pulled the trigger of his automatic.

BLAM!!!

The slug tore into Harlow mid-chest. He stumbled back a step and looked down at the crimson stream gushing from him. The expression on his face was bewilderment.

Charlie snatched the Rossi off the bar. He turned and fired.

BLAM!!!

The wild shot hit Harlow in the back, ripping through his spinal column.

"Aw, *shit!*" Moreno said, as he watched the key to his grand design pitch forward onto the carpet. He glowered at Eddie.

The stunned henchman attempted an apology, but the words wouldn't form.

Charlie didn't wait to gloat over Harlow. He didn't wait for his gut to coach him either. "*Move!*" he told himself,   "Get the fuck out of here."

He barreled out of the den, heading for the front door.

"Get him!" he heard Moreno snap.

The door was locked. Charlie's moist fingers struggled with the deadbolt.

BLAM!!!

A slug from Eddie's .45 punched a hole in the door, three inches from Charlie's head.

Charlie dove to the floor.

BLAM!!! BLAM!!!

He fired two quick shots at Eddie. The bullets splintered the paneling, forcing the big man to retreat into the den.

Charlie spotted the French doors at the back of the living room. On the other side was that large dark rolling lawn. There was a cabaña out there, and a tennis court and swimming pool. Places to hide.

BLAM!!!

He fired another round at the den entrance, as he dashed through the living room. "Vin fucking Diesel," he shouted, covering his face with his hands.

He crashed through the French doors. Glass shattered in every direction.

Charlie hit the concrete terrace hard. Ignoring the glass and wood splinters that sliced his body, he scrambled to his feet and jumped off the terrace into the expansive blackness of lawn below. "*Shit!*" he muttered, hitting his knee on a sprinkler head. He scooted through some shrubbery and leaned against the base of the terrace.

"There's a light switch in there." he heard Moreno say five feet above him. Seconds later, the lawn was flooded with light, all coming from lampposts surrounding the estate.

Charlie saw that his protective shadows had been washed away. He knew he had to move...*fast*. He cocked the Rossi and broke from his hiding place, limping toward the pool and cabaña.

"There he goes!" Moreno shouted.

Charlie heard the two hoods scrambling down the steps behind him. He threw a glance over his shoulder. Eddie had dropped down on one knee, and was taking aim with his .45.

BLAM!!!

A sharp hot pain grabbed Charlie by the hip and caused him to stumble. "*Fuck!*" he screamed. The Rossi flew out of his hand, as he hit the ground. He tried to clamber to his feet.

BLAM!!!

A "hammer" struck him on the side of the head. He went down again. There were no final thoughts this time, as the darkness engulfed him.

Eddie, his weapon cocked, rushed across the lawn toward the lifeless figure. "Finish him off," Moreno said, hurrying along behind him.

Half a dozen yards from Powers, Eddie froze. His face whitened. "*Jesus Christ!*" He stared at a spot ten feet above the body.

"What the fuck's wrong?" Moreno snapped, reaching his frightened henchman's side.

"L...Look!" Eddie managed to stammer. "D...Don't ya s...see it!?!" He pointed at the transparent specter floating above Powers' immobile form, connected to it by a thin white cord.

"What're you pointing at?" Moreno was unable to perceive what Eddie was babbling about. All *he* saw above the body was empty air.

Eddie panicked. He raised his automatic and pointed it at the phantom.

BLAM!!! BLAM!!!

"It's still there." he shouted. "Let's scram!"

Moreno grabbed the .45 from Eddie and cocked it. "Stop wasting time," he said, aiming it downward at Powers' body.

"This is the police." The voice from the bullhorn turned Moreno on his heel. He spotted three...no, four black S.W.A.T. uniforms on the terrace. Each man had a high-powered rifle pointed in his direction. "Drop your weapons. *Now!*"

"There's a back way out," Moreno shouted to Eddie. The two hoods turned and began sprinting across the lawn toward the pool area.

BLAM!!! BLAM!!!

Moreno felt the two rifle bullets whiz past his ear. He didn't want to die. He stopped running, dropped the .45 and raised his hands above his head.

Eddie scooped the weapon up from the ground. Out of the corner of his eye, he saw a S.W.A.T. officer racing in his direction. He aimed the .45 to bring the man down.

BLAM!!!

The shot from the officer's rifle caught Eddie in the windpipe. He plopped down onto his rear end, gasping for air.

Hal Stuart stood on the terrace, watching the pockets of activity on the lawn below him. Two S.W.A.T. officers were handcuffing Freddy Moreno. They'd read the son-of-a-bitch his rights, then take him downtown and charge him with first degree murder. With lethal injection hanging over his head, Stuart figured the slime ball might be willing to sing some pretty sweet songs to the Federal Crime Commission. He felt good about that.

He looked a few yards away and saw the coroner's men bagging up the remains of Eddie Clarkson, heist man, hit man, racketeer. He felt good about that, too.

He shifted his attention to Agent McNally, approaching him from the house. "There's some reporters and television crews out front," he said. "They want to know about Harlow."

"I'll talk to them," Stuart said. "Tell them to wait."

"What *was* the Harlow/Moreno connection?" he wondered. There had to be *something* there. Otherwise, why would the Texas hood have been in the California gubernatorial candidate's home? He figured that those answers would be forthcoming within the next few weeks.

He looked back down to the lawn and saw Miles Goodman standing by the Bradshaw girl. He didn't feel good about her. She was sweet and naive. And, there she was, kneeling on the lawn next to that smart-assed petty crook while the paramedics worked over him.

"Powers, you bastard," Stuart mused, "did you *really* have that fucking out-of-body experience? Or, was it all just another one of your jokes?"

He wondered if the world would be better off without Charlie Powers. The sad thing," he thought, "is that, with a girl like Jenny Bradshaw, ol' Charlie might've gone straight."

Stuart decided that he wasn't needed there any longer. Time to deal with the press. He walked back through the broken French doors.

Jenny shifted her kneeling position on the lawn. She stroked Charlie's face, careful not to disturb the blood-soaked bandages. "Charlie," she said, holding back her tears, "please, open your eyes."

Charlie didn't move.

The black paramedic took the stethoscope away from his chest. He looked up at Goodman, shook his head and shrugged.

Miles stuck his hands in his pockets, and then shifted the weight on his feet. Behind him, he saw two men coming toward them with a gurney. "Jenny," he said, "the ambulance is here."

"I don't want to leave him."

The paramedic's voice was gentle. "I think he's gone, Miss."

"*No!*" she screamed. "*Charlie!*" She brushed Goodman's comforting hand away from her shoulder. Her tone turned angry. "Charlie, I flew all the way here from Dallas. Don't you *dare* die on me!"

She began to weep. Goodman gestured to the paramedics. They moved away to give her some privacy.

"Charlie," she cried, "I want you in my life." Her body began to convulse with sobs.

Something stroked her arm. She glanced over and saw Charlie's bandaged hand touching her.

———

233

"How come," he said, opening his eyes, "whenever we meet, you're crying?"

Jenny beamed a teary smile. She reached down and hugged him.

"Ouch!" he said.

THE END